The Cold, Black Sea

Ghost Stories

Campbell Hart

The Sniper

"In no-man's land, the only way to live is to accept that you're already dead."

1

The bullets buzzed like bees, the barrage turned the sky black, with men reduced to a puff of crimson in the blink of an eye. I watched, powerless, as the second wave advanced. The relentless strafing from the enemy trenches ripped apart the steady advance of our assault. The neat lines of Haig's offensive quickly broke down when the slow ordered walk-through was staggered by the crump holes left by our own heavy artillery. But for those approaching the first objective, it only got worse, and I found it difficult to stay focused when the men came in sight of the German front line. The machine guns showed no pity and the typewriters rapped out 100 shells a second, decimating our ranks in a mechanical heartbeat, depleting our numbers by hundreds every single minute.

I suppose I should have thought myself lucky. I, Jim West, had been approached to join the new Scouting, Observation and Sniping School. I'd worked as a ghillie for a time before the war, and I knew how to shoot. The top brass were looking to redress the balance. They said we needed to find a way to stop the chippy German snipers in their tracks; they had been picking us off with alarming monotony since the war began. At first we thought the deadly head shots were just flukes, but we didn't know they had telescopic sights. Looking out over the Somme it seemed there was a lot we didn't know.

Stationed in a forward position I was waiting for a counter attack that never came. The Boche stood firm and defended well. It was too much for some, and the faint-hearted, overwhelmed by the situation, tried to turn and run. But the whippers-in had their measure and they snapped away at their backs, using pistols to enforce their orders. Those who dared to dissent didn't last long and I'm sad to say that I saw a few men shot down by our own officers that day. Poor sods. But there was a certain karma about that battle, and the last line of defence provided no special protection for the officers either. I watched one Captain try to harry a Private back into the fray. He was a big man, muscular and fast, but hot lead knows no fear and moments later he was gone too. I had been screaming out for them to take cover, but of course they couldn't hear me. There was nothing else for it so I continued to fire, picking off anyone in range, with my expertise in high demand. But after the heat of battle, there was nothing I could do but wait.

I'd been in position since the night before. Dug-in deep and heavily camouflaged, I was tasked with taking out my opposite number in the trenches over no-man's land. It had seemed a simple enough task on paper, but in practice was easier said than done. Our main problem was that our rifles weren't up to the job, we were years behind the Germans. When our snipers first began to ply their trade the officers demanded high standards, and the dress code called for full military dress. Men were sent out into battle in their oversized service caps, with the broad peaked brim marking them out as easy targets; most didn't last the day.

You see, the Germans have a system. They dig in, using sandbagged walls with angled firing slots. Some of them are so bold you wouldn't believe it; they lie out in the battlefield using shell holes and metal plates for cover. If you saw the flash of the shot, nine times out of ten you'd be dead already.

But there were no German snipers today and it was now the turn of enemy shells to respond to our week-long barrage of their defences.

The low velocity shells were the worst. First came the whistle in the distance and if you were dim enough to hang around, you could watch as they sought you out. God help you if you got caught in the blast.

The noise was deafening and constant, the roar of battle eventually tapered away to a high pitched tone as the world passed by in a blur; hour after hour of non-stop destruction. The screams of the dying pierced the cacophony of death, as shells rained down. The lucky ones died straight away or vanished completely, but the shrapnel left a wave of carnage that would leave some of us screaming for days.

It hadn't always been like that.

April 1916

When we first arrived on the Somme it had been a beautiful day, and a far cry from the horror that followed. The low, rolling hills still looked like farmland; the lush green pastures intoxicated our city lungs with sweet summer smells, while the burning sun made it feel like paradise.

Our battalion was relieving the French who it seemed, on first inspection, had been playing it quiet. They had it all worked out nice and cushy alright. It was less of a war to them and more of a gentleman's agreement. I could hardly believe it when they told me their routine. There were three bombardments a day; two shells at 10, 2 and 5; with the Boche replying in timely fashion. The risks were few and it seemed as if no-one really cared; they liked their lazy war. But it didn't stay civilised for long. The changing of the guard meant that British military discipline was enforced in double time. We weren't here to muck around, there was a war to fight which suited me just fine. I wanted to win and leave, to get this over with and return home a hero.

***

We settled in quickly and it wasn't long before the artillery arrived and the ground soon became pockmarked with shells and the greenery blackened. Sorties were still few but we were building up to something big; we all knew that, and we couldn't wait to get started.

It was around this time that we first heard of the infamous sniper. I'd come across an aged French soldier of around forty-something, who recounted an old wives tale that he took great delight in the telling of. He was preparing to be redeployed to the north and we'd shared a bottle of whisky behind the lines, in a village called Albert. In the distance a golden statue of Mary and the baby Jesus sat precariously on top of a local church that had been hit by shell fire. The effigy had fallen over 90 degrees, and was hanging on, a hundred feet up, supported by a few straining metal wires. I kept glancing at it absentmindedly, half expecting it to crash back to earth, as my host tried his very best to unnerve me. He told me of a phantom sniper, the one they called 'Oeil Mort' or Dead Eye to you and me.

'Do you take me for a fool?' I swigged back the whisky, keeping my eyes on the Frenchman. His company had been fine at first although the language barrier made for rather painful conversation.

'But no, you must listen. This phantom, he has killed 45 of our men these last six months. If you are out on patrol, there is no knowing where the shot will come from.' He stopped to look around. I wondered if he was embarrassed that one of his countrymen might hear him. "No-one ever sees the shot, but men flop down.' He clapped his hands together in case I was as slow-witted as he. 'Bang, then it's like they sleep. You know?'

I was pretty sure the old-timer was well soused by this time, and taking something of a liberty with my good nature. He'd relaxed with every shot and it seemed as if there was no way to stop this ridiculous chatter. I'd shared the best part of my only bottle of Grants with him, keen to learn the secrets of our new position before we were thrust into action. Instead I was being fed superstition. I was growing impatient and decided it was time to leave.

'If you don't mind my saying so, it sounds like you should stay off the sauce, old man. It obviously doesn't agree with you.'

But my drinking partner was unmoved. As I laughed he shook his head, a new anger had gripped him. 'You wait, monsieur. This one, he never misses, and he cannot be found, so he cannot be killed. Is this a man? I think not; no way.'

I could see that he was gripping his glass too tightly, his knuckles white with the force of it. It seemed ridiculous to me that we might come to blows over nonsense like this, when there was so much work to do. I decided to try to calm him before things got out of hand.

'The Germans are good snipers, I'll grant you that. But rest assured, there is no phantom, it's no ghost that kills your men.'

He snorted and left, muttering a string of words I could not understand, but suspected were not entirely complimentary. I never saw him again.

2

Glasgow - August 1914

I'd signed up in the first wave of volunteers with two of my oldest friends. We became part of the 1st Glasgow Tram Battalion and were treated like heroes at home in the Gorbals.

I'd known Harry Lovett and Charlie Balfour all my days. We all lived in the same tenement and grew up together, our lives interlocked by the narrowness of our shared community. As boys we ran the streets terrorising our neighbours, consoled ourselves through school, before leaving as soon as we could. Today we worked at the same depot and we were happy enough. We had never had cause to question our existence until now.

Enlisting had been a spur of the moment thing. We were at Ibrox watching Rangers where it was still goalless with Hamilton Accies in the opening game of the season. It was less than two weeks after Asquith had declared war on Germany and it was all we could talk about, as the game slogged-on in the background.

I'd been thinking about signing-up for a few days although I hadn't discussed it with anyone. Even so, I could see there was potential for us to join up as a group and I wanted to push the point, 'I was reading the paper today. It said that they're looking for volunteers. Maybe we should all join up; together, all three of us?'

Charlie Balfour had a face on him like he had just put his hand in a manky bedpan, 'Are you daft, Jim? What about our jobs? We were lucky to get on the books at the depot. Do you think I want to give all that up to go to war?'

Needless to say this wasn't the response I wanted to hear. Charlie Balfour had always been a bit of a coward. He'd need to be convinced that this was the right thing to do. In the background a sudden cheer signalled the only goal of the game.

I raised my voice to be heard over the noise of the crowd, 'If we don't volunteer now and go over and get this sorted out, do you know what will happen?' Charlie was shaking his head, while Harry was back watching the game. They were losing interest.

'We need to be the ones to set an example, or they'll be over here next. The Germans will be in Glasgow and we'll be part of their

13

empire. It's what they want. I read it in the paper. They see what we've got, and they want it for themselves. That's why they're building the dreadnoughts. Massive gunboats like that and they've barely got a coast. You both need to wise up.'

Harry Lovett was laughing, 'The bloody Prussians are no match for the British Empire. If they come at us we'll swat them away like flies. There's nothing to worry about, and there's certainly no need for us to rush to war before we're needed.'

He knew how to wind me up, did Harry, but I wouldn't be brow beaten on this one. I knew his father had been in service in Africa and I knew exactly how to needle him, 'Like the Boers, you mean? We showed them a thing or too.'

Harry was shaking his head, trying not to rise to it, but as usual he couldn't help himself, 'That was a mistake. And you don't become the greatest country in the world by not making a few mistakes along the way. The Germans are not in the same class as we are. I mean look around. You're living in the second city of the British Empire. We build the ships that rule the waves. We're the greatest nation on earth and our army will make short work of this war. You wait and see.'

Harry had gone red in the face. I knew he didn't really believe what he was saying; recent history didn't back him up, 'You're wrong, Harry. We need to go and do our bit, and we need to go now, while we still can. Think about it man, we'd come back as heroes. Better still, we'd get out of Glasgow too; see a bit of the world. We've spent our whole lives here and you know fine well that we'll die here too. There's no opportunities for the likes of us.' I had the attention of both of them now. They knew what I was saying was true. 'I hear that France is hot. Hot and dry. It would make a change from this.' I pointed to the skies as the heaven's opened to help me to make my point. 'What do you think, Charlie?' He'd been quieter than usual; hadn't said a word, in fact.

But Harry spoke for him, 'Don't mind him, Jim. He's gone soft on Alice Simpson.' Harry was punching Charlie in the arm but was still getting no response. I laughed along as we wrestled in the stands. Charlie pushed back eventually, indignant at his manhandling, 'Ach, boys, but I like her don't I? I'm not sure if I could go to war.' He was staring at his feet and couldn't meet our gaze. 'I'm jumpy enough as it is. I've never been in as much as a fist fight let alone a full blown war.' He stood leaning against the metal terracing with his head in hands, 'I mean, how long would we be away for?'

I sensed it was time to reel them in. There had been a definite shift in attitude. Truth be told, I didn't want to go alone. I put my hand on Charlie's shoulder. 'It would be no time at all, pal. Less than a year, maybe not even that long. We could do this, we really could, but I don't want to leave Glasgow without you two idiots, now do I?'

The topic wasn't mentioned for the rest of the day and in Samson's bar that night we drank our weight in whisky. As we staggered home a pact was made that we would protect each other through thick and thin, and the very next morning we dragged ourselves out of our beds and sloped off to Queen Street to sign-up for King and Country.

***

A few weeks later we marched up Sauchiehall Street in our thousands to the beat of Scotland the Brave. The city centre was rammed with people who had turned out to cheer us on. We strode up the hill to Lauders corner and back down to Central Station, with pride in our hearts and hope for the future. The thick khaki uniforms still felt stiff but we felt smart in our tartan trews and united in a common cause. As we marched together, side-by-side; me, Harry and Charlie felt like kings. The girls waved from the sidelines and our mothers wept at the station. By the time we rolled out of our home city we were on cloud nine. By God, the Germans were in for a surprise.

As we raised a glass to the success of our great endeavour, we did so in blissful ignorance.

April 1916

As I said before, by the time we reached the Somme it wasn't half bad. The war hadn't really touched the landscape and the pastures had mostly escaped the fury which had transformed the Ardennes and Ypres, places that we'd already seen more than enough of. There were trenches, of course, but they weren't sophisticated; crude burrows dug into the ground, with little in the way of shoring up for heavy defence. The thick chalky clay meant the walls looked solid enough to the naked eye, but if they were shelled they collapsed immediately. It was a dangerous game to play.

On arrival, the communications trench took us through the middle of a farm house, an odd sight that I will always remember. The Frenchies had dug right through the house and both floors were exposed, with curtains flapping through glassless frames, the furniture untouched. But strange as it was, it would be the events that followed that would leave a lasting legacy on my young mind.

As the weeks passed the rumours of the dead eyed sniper persisted, and it wasn't long before we got our first taste of the legendary 'phantom'. We had mocked the French for their superstition, but they had got one thing right. You never saw where the shots came from, and the marksman never missed.

June 1916

On my first night raid my orders were to take prisoners from the enemy trench, which was something I thought little of at the time. We were there to do a job and the Boche rarely moved. They were dug in deep, well prepared, and waiting. It frustrated us that we couldn't draw them out to engage with us in the open. I reasoned that if they wouldn't come to us then we'd simply turn the tables. 'Old Gerry had better be ready; he's going to have company tonight.'

The privates pulled back the massed coils of barbed wire and we were given the order to move out. Low and slow we went, heads down and sloping through the mud. The Huns shot out red flares at regular intervals which robbed us of the cover of night and marked us out as targets for anyone looking, and there was always someone. It seemed like Gerry never slept.

We were spotted having gone less than fifty yards, with the bright red flare light picking us out as sitting ducks. I swore loudly as the typewriters opened up and splutted through the muck, ten feet in front of us. But we were too quick that time and threw ourselves in a flooded crump-hole. But the onslaught continued, and the steady rattle of bullets soon gave way to artillery which crept ever closer to our sanctuary.

We were powerless, and for what seemed like hours the ground shook around us. The noise became unbearable and I sat and screamed, curled up in a ball, half submerged in filthy water. I could feel my body start to sink into the mud. I heard the shell and watched as it hurtled towards me. I braced myself and expected to die. One second passed and then four more, but the explosion didn't come. Turning from the earthen wall I'd been embracing I saw the shell's metal casing had become lodged in the side of the crater. Thank God for a dud! But not everyone had been lucky. The shell had sliced through one of my party and left him in pieces; his dismembered corpse was floating all around me. There were no signs of life anywhere near the crater.

I heard the noise before I realised that the danger hadn't passed. The shell was hissing and I knew I had to leave; another stray bullet would be all it took to finish the job. The mission had failed so I reasoned it was safe to return to base. I could not continue alone. Pulling myself slowly over the rim of the crater I felt heavy with water. Back in no-man's land I started to run. I had no other choice.

What happened next is hard to recall, it seemed like a dream. There was no let-up in the barrage and the world around me was shrouded in the smog of war so I couldn't be sure if I was heading in the right direction. As I ran, heavy and tired with the weight of my waterlogged clothes, I glanced left. I thought I'd seen something out of the corner of my eye. Yes there it is again. A figure in the distance, way out into no-man's land. It was a sniper, rising from his nest, clothed in white with black markings to make him blend in to the background. He was running towards me, with his rifle aimed low with bullets firing in quick succession. He was shouting something I couldn't make out. Again and again he said the same thing. 'SICH VERSACHANZEN, SICH VERSACHANZEN,' I didn't know what it meant and I didn't mean to find out, so I kept on running and didn't look back.

My movement felt slow and laboured. The seconds hung heavy as I hauled myself to the next hole some twenty yards distant. I suddenly felt very cold, and I could have sworn someone had touched me. The voice rang out again, 'SICH VERSACHANZEN, ODER STIRB,' but when I looked back there was no-one there. I kept running. In my head I could still hear that terrible voice.

I stayed out in the filth of no-man's land for two days. Pinned down and unable to move I defended my position the best that I could. Through the haze of the battlefield I fired at distant figures that scuttled like insects from hole to hole looking for cover. My only goal was to try and stay alive. Time and time again I hit my mark. Pinned down and with no rations they told me I was raving when they found me, covered in mud in an abandoned trench.

3

Harry Lovett was there when I woke up. He sat, cap in hand, staring at the floor. I still felt dazed.

'Where am I?' A blur of bodies flashed past as I tried to take in the room. I was finding it difficult to focus

'You alright there, Jim boy? I thought we'd lost you.'

Looking around I realised that I was in field hospital that had been rigged up in a large church. Light pierced through the stained glass window, with golden shafts tapering across the huddled mass of casualties which made up the captive congregation. My first thought was that I must have been injured, but how? I started to check my body for souvenirs but everything seemed OK.

'What's going on?'

'You're fine, Jim. Everything's still there and in perfect working order.' Harry was smiling now; he seemed pleased to see me. 'You were in a bad way when they found you though. You were screaming the place down.'

After the death of my mother I'd never been back in a hospital. I didn't like them and looking around I remembered why. And yet, despite the injuries and the pungent smell of open wounds, there was little in the way of audible complaint. People had surrendered to their fate and lived on in hope that time might magically rewind; they'd be disappointed on that front.

In the background I became aware of a steady rumble that was gently shaking the building. The lights swayed slightly with every new contact and dust sieved down from the exposed wooden rafters. Harry bent forward and touched my arm. He could see I was worried.

'You look like you've seen a ghost, Jim. Are you feeling OK?'

I said I was fine but I wasn't, far from it. Thinking back I tried to remember what had happened, but all I could glimpse were fragments. 'Why am I here, Harry? I'm not injured, am I?' I couldn't remember being brought in. 'I need to get out of here, back to the line, before they start asking questions about why I didn't come back.' I was clawing at the bed sheets. I'd seen what they did to cowards and I hadn't come all this way to be shot by my own men.

I needed to leave and it was obvious something was happening not far off, 'What's that noise outside, are we under attack?'

'Hey, hey, easy there fella; it's OK. You did well to survive for so long out there. You got caught in a barrage; the biggest one yet. We could see you firing off shots for days. But you were erratic, and the screaming was drawing heavy fire. You kept shouting that you were a sniper and to take cover, but the Germans weren't listening.'

I still couldn't remember, 'What happened to the rest of them, Harry? Who else made it back?'

Harry slumped back against his seat and exhaled in one long, resigned breath. I knew the answer before he opened his mouth.

'It was just you. No-one else was there.'

'They let you come looking for me?'

'It doesn't work like that and you know it. They wanted to get you back behind the lines, to save you from the Germans. It was a miracle you made it back at all. They'll be writing a book about you soon, my man. You were hopping from crater to crater and the bastards couldn't pin you down. You've become quite a legend.'

'A legend?' I asked, still trying to remember what had driven me to survive, something I simply could not recall.

'No-one is more surprised than me you old rogue,' Harry was laughing; he seemed more at ease. God knows what the doctors had told him. He moved the conversation on to the here and now, 'Don't fret about it, Jim. There's not much happening with Gerry today. Our artillery is pounding the lines.' He was pantomiming guns, pumping his hands back and forth with his fingers pointed at the ceiling, 'Big 60 pounders and every howitzer we've got is giving the Boche merry hell. I should think it will only be a matter of time before we get ready for the Big Push.'

'I can't stay here, Harry. I need to be part of it; it's why we came out here in the first place. Don't let them hold me.'

'You're not being held here, Jim. Like I said, you're a hero; your antics out there have really raised morale. You'll be out there, don't worry, but for God's sake give yourself time to recover. You were very near enemy lines when they found you. Amazing really; you'd used everything you had to fend them off. You're lucky to be alive.'

'Lucky to be alive,' I said it out loud to try and feel the words, but there was nothing.

'I'll see you later.' Harry stood ringing his cap in his hands. I could see he still had doubts about me. But I nodded all the same and Harry left. Before long I had drifted off into a fitful sleep.

In my dreams I was back in no-man's land. I stood naked in the mud and peered through the mist. There was something out there, shrouded and hidden; something malignant that meant me harm. For although I couldn't see it; I could feel its intent. Rounds cracked off intermittently in the background, the fog changing colour from time-to-time as flares cut through the night sky. I saw the outline first, nothing more than the suggestion of a figure. I was breathing, heavy and hard, my anxiety rising. It was still summer, but I could see my breath expel and linger before me, as if the temperature had dropped rapidly. It felt like time had slowed to a snail's pace. It was then that the words came, ringing out through the still of the night. A familiar, voice; yet distorted, and grim.

'SICH VERSACHANZEN, ODER STIRB.'

I looked ahead and behind, but I could see nothing. Then the voice came again, and this time I understood.

'TAKE COVER, OR DIE.'

It was turning back that I saw him. A figure clad in loose white sacking, greased with oil, the camouflage gear used to obscure snipers in the chalky soil of the Somme. I was rooted to the spot and watched in horror as he started to run directly at me. Rifle clenched at the hip with his ammunition bag swinging behind him, dragging through the mud.

'TAKE COVER, OR DIE,' he screamed.

My ears hurt with the volume of the voice, every time the warning came was louder again, a glottal rasp, cutting through the gloom. I couldn't move. I knew my time was up. The last thing I saw was a flash of light, and then I felt the bullet pierce my temple, releasing me from my living hell.

'Jesus,' I sat bolt upright, screaming for safety. I was back in the hospital, but drenched in sweat. It had felt so real and as I gingerly reached to feel my forehead I expected to find a wound, but of course, there was nothing. Outside the bombardment continued. I sighed and tried to go back to sleep, thankful for my sanctuary.

***

There was no let-up in the barrage and I was released from hospital the next day and billeted five miles behind the lines. All leave was cancelled so I knew we were getting ready for an attack. They said they needed every man they could get and that after my amazing feats it would be good for the men to see a real soldier going back out to watch their backs. Given my training I was earmarked for sniper duty, tasked with taking out the German machine gunners. I didn't have much time left to prepare, so I sought out Harry at his observation post.

We talked about little things, about pubs in Glasgow and girls we'd known, both keen to avoid dwelling on the task at hand. Thinking of home, I realised I hadn't seen Charlie for a few days and asked Harry if he'd spoken with him.

Harry looked back at me, puzzled, 'I thought he was with you, Jim? When you were out on the mission to bring back prisoners. You would both have been caught in the barrage, don't you remember?'

I didn't. Thinking back, I still only had a vague notion about what had happened, the details of the mission eluded me. How many were there on the patrol, seven or eight? Could Charlie really have been one of them?

'I don't remember much about it, Harry. I wish I could.'

A nervousness gripped me. I tried to recall what had happened. A flash of crimson came to mind; the noise of persistent shells. A new landscape was forming, as the ground burst open to reveal another crater, the whirl of shrapnel whizzing past my head – another lucky escape. Men disappeared like magic – there one minute, then nothing. But was Charlie there too? I simply did not know.

'I think you've got it wrong, Harry; Charlie wasn't there that night. I would have remembered that.'

Harry was shaking his head, 'I know it was a tough shift out there. God knows how you survived, but I watched you both leave for the assembly trenches that night. I wished you luck.' Harry was finding it hard to look me in the eyes and had turned away. 'It just wasn't Charlie's night. And that's something that you are just going to have to accept.'

I sensed what he was getting at, 'It wasn't my fault that he died.'

'So you do remember?'

I couldn't, but Harry seemed so convinced. I could sense his disgust. It was so frustrating not to know.

'All I remember is that my patrol was cut apart out there. I didn't know what way was up. We were running blind and under heavy attack. I stayed put and tried to fend them off. The only people out there were Gerry patrols. They tried to take me down but I wouldn't let them.'

'Gerry patrols?' Harry seemed angry. He had stopped what he was doing and had squared up in front of me.

'Aye, Gerry patrols. There were a lot of men out there, looking for me. I could see them, but I kept shooting. That's why I'm here.'

'The barrage was ours, Jim.' There were tears in his Harry's eyes, something I hadn't seen before. I was confused; there was something he wasn't telling me. 'You were out there for days and didn't come back. There's no way the Boche launched an attack when we were throwing everything we had at them. They simply couldn't have survived.'

'Are you calling me a liar?'

'I've been on point, Jim. There was no-one out there but you.'

'That's ridiculous. I saw the patrols with my own eyes.'

Harry's eyes shone with tears, his voice trembled as he tried to look me in the eyes, but had to look past me, 'I don't know what you saw, Jim, but Charlie's gone. There's nothing left, so whatever it is that happened out there, I don't want to know. It's just you and me now and we promised to see each other through this, just in case you had forgotten.'

Harry turned and left. I felt that I was running out of time to find the answers that I needed, but they just wouldn't come. It wasn't long after, that our orders came in.

Tomorrow was to be the day of the Big Push, which meant that I only had a few hours before I would have to leave. I settled back in my dugout, and tried to wait out my allotted time. With no sleep, there were only nightmares ahead of me.

4

July 1st, 1916

The bombardment of the German forward positions had lasted for a week and we were all convinced that we had ground them down to dust. After two years of monotonous waiting, fighting, recovery and rebuilding, the men were getting ready to move; we sensed we were finally on the verge of a major breakthrough. Our skirmishes on the Somme front had been piecemeal up to that point, and the massed battalions were all itching to see some real action. The largess of our bombardment had everyone in high spirits. The rank and file laughed nervously as the rum rations were passed round in the assembly trenches. They explained that the open ground was badly churned, and the infantry were instructed not to run; that they should preserve their strength to overwhelm the remaining resistance. We'd all been told that this would be a day to remember.

They were right.

My day started earlier than most. Under the cover of darkness I had crept back out into no-man's land to take up my position. The idea was simple; to pick off enemy machine gun and sniping positions, and to stay alive for as long as I could while the offensive pushed forward. I wasn't alone, of course, and there were around twenty of us spread out along the line.

I had picked out my spot early on. About forty yards off the German line there was a natural dip in the terrain which had already been sandbagged by the enemy. They'd been using it to foil one of our tunnelling attempts some weeks back, but the wall worked just as well in reverse, and the position would give me a wide angle vista of the section of the enemy trench that my battalion would be attacking.

When I arrived I saw that I already had company of the dear departed kind. A dead sniper lay on the other side of the wall and was blocking my shot. It was dark enough that I still had time to move the body. If I didn't I'd need to find a new spot somewhere out in the open, and if I did that, I'd be signing my own death warrant.

The sniper, still in full camouflage, was heavy and I struggled to move him. His stiff bones cracked in protest when they were prised from their resting place. I didn't need to move the body far, though, and stopped for a moment to catch my breath.

It was getting light and I wouldn't be able to stand exposed for much longer. On closer inspection I found that the sandbagged wall was covered in the blood of my current burden, but through the blotted spread I noticed crudely written words. Peering through the half-darkness, I saw it was German; hard to read in the dim light. The message probably passed for the last words of the man I was grappling with.

The letters were bloated and had lost form through the fabric of the sandbags, but they were words I knew.

SICH VERSACHANZEN, ODER STIRB

'Take cover, or die,' I whispered, cowed into a fearful lull. Suddenly there was a flash of light. The body of the dead sniper seemed to move. He turned and was whole again, his decayed corpse filling out, as if his death was being reversed. I pulled at his cowl which slipped off to reveal eyes that had been burned out by shafts of light, which shone still from his sockets. The unnatural heat bore into me and then he was gone. The body of the sniper simply fell away, leaving me holding the rags of his uniform and nothing more. I was hyperventilating and tried to breathe, but a fog consumed me before my life fell into darkness. After that I felt nothing at all.

***

Somehow, I endured. When I came to I was still in position. A thick mist had settled on the Somme, weather that would give me natural cover when the time came to open fire. How soon till dawn now? I kept checking my watch as if the very act would hurry the world to meet my schedule. I knew I didn't have long to wait, but it seemed like an eternity.

I had mixed emotions that day. I was excited that we could soon blast through the front line and split the army ahead of us, but there were nerves nonetheless. It had been a strange few days and my memory was still fogged from my exile; stranded and helpless in the most dangerous place on earth. To be back again so soon, gave me no comfort whatsoever.

***

When the signal came it was both shocking and huge. At 7.28am there was such an explosion as I have ever experienced. When the Lochnager mine went up it felt like the Lord God almighty had swept the Somme with all his rage. The force of the blast was extraordinary; so vicious that I cracked off a shot by mistake. No-one could have heard it, though, the sound dwarfed by the crescendo of earth that was being forced up by the blast, hundreds of feet in the air. Later they'd say the explosion could be heard in London. All we cared about was putting fear into Gerry's hearts, and I'm sure we had achieved at least that. Ten minutes later, men swarmed over the top of our trenches. I sensed victory was near.

Harry Lovett was fired up.

Hot with rum and the nervous energy we all carried before an attack I entered a kind of suspended state, driven purely by adrenalin and the knowledge that only luck would see me return to base that night. At first there was little sound on the battlefield, but so many men as would do your heart proud. Tens of thousands of us seethed over the top and made our way up the hill towards the ruined German trenches.

We had been expecting an easy day of it. We outnumbered the Germans by five to one and we were convinced our rout would be absolute. But we couldn't have been more wrong. The counter attack started almost immediately. The surprise on the men's faces was palpable; no-one expected resistance.

As the front row fell and the second was cut apart, the men behind started to waver; this hadn't been part of the plan. I wished I was with Jim West now; I found his calmness under fire reassuring. He was supposed to be out here already, but as the carnage continued I wondered if he would even have made it into position. I turned to look back at the safety behind only to be faced with a shaking Captain. He was standing with his pistol pointing at my face. 'Turn around,' he screamed, 'Turn around and keep walking.'

I called out for Jim, begged him to pick off our tormentors, but I was on my own. There was a single shot. Out of the corner of my eye I thought I saw a figure dart off in the background. I saw a flash of light and the Captain beside me was dead. It was then that the typewriters opened up from a concealed position in no-man's land, and we were cut down like daisies in a field.

What we hoped would be a leisurely stroll, quickly become a death march. Somehow the Germans were ready. God knows how they did it, but they were making short work of us. The front ranks rushed forward as best they could, but they ended up either tangled in the wire, or cut to pieces. The mud ran red with the blood of the 15th, and when the shells started we knew that we didn't stand a chance. The day was lost.

***

When I awoke it was night time. I felt a great weight on me, and for a second I couldn't move. I realised that my face was half buried in mud and as I tried to breathe I found myself choking on loose earth. I pushed down with both hands and used my back to try to move the burden above. Inch by inch it gave way and then, suddenly, the pressure was gone. Rising to my knees I found myself in a shell hole. There were maybe a dozen dead soldiers in this makeshift grave. I'd been pinned down by three bodies that looked to have been thrown in from the battlefield. The soldiers were all basket cases, barely recognisable as people, with limbs missing and their humanity stripped away. I struggled to free myself from my hellish bedfellows, and pushed myself back until I came to rest on other side of the hollow. In the distance I heard the rasp of a flare, the noise giving prior warning of the dangers that would follow. On the other side of the trench I could see that I had company, someone sitting just like me.

'Hey, you there; are you wounded?'

But he didn't answer and as the blood red skies grew brighter with the latest flare I saw why. Although the man looked whole from a distance, he was anything but. He'd been hit by shrapnel, with his head severed from just above his eye line. He sat there still, with a cigarette in his mouth, as if waiting for a light. Patient in his oblivion, it seemed he might yet stand up and walk around.

What to do? I could wait and hope to be relieved, but I stood an equal chance of being discovered by a German patrol, and they wouldn't be taking prisoners on a day like today. Perhaps, if I could get back to our lines with intelligence on the state of the enemy positions, the information would buy me a day or two away from this carnage. How could our plans have been so wrong? It was like Gerry knew we were coming.

I finally plucked up enough courage to peer out from the crater's ridge, but I wasn't prepared for the sight that greeted me. From my position and towards the front line there were too many men to count. Thousands lay dead and dying, dull moans signalling that for many their long fight was almost at an end as they bled out in the mud. In the distance I could see the sorry buggers mangled in barbed wire. Some had been ripped apart by the machine guns, with only shredded uniforms to mark the men that had started out that day. Bodies were piled up, three and four deep in places. I covered my eyes, hoping that the simple gesture might wipe the horror from my memory. It seemed that we'd stuck to our orders and continued our slow advance, but there was no chance of making it through against firepower like that. Looking back was a similar scene. Wave after wave had been dispatched on permanent leave, and I don't mind admitting that I struggled to take in the scale of the carnage. So many lives cut short.

I'm not sure how long I sat there but it was getting light, just before sunset. The early morning fog clung thickly to the ground; its swirling eddies partially masking the scale of the death around me. I became aware of the gentle buzz of a blue bottle that had come to rest on a body not far from my crater. The flesh was ripped and red, an easy meal for this gorging parasite. Then, in the distance I saw someone moving through the gloom. Surely no-one would be brazen enough to walk through this, as if it was a stroll in the park, but yes, here he comes – walking slowly towards me. He was tall and he stalked through the bodies, aiming his rifle from the hip, while his ammunition belt dragged carelessly through the killing field.

'TAKE COVER' he bellowed. I couldn't believe he'd be so bold.

'Not so loud,' I said. 'You'll give the game away. Do you want to wake up Gerry?' I was more concerned for my own safety than his, although it seemed the two were now intertwined. And I was right, it was too late. Someone on the line had heard us, and the firing began in earnest. I knew I couldn't stay and turned to run. Making a bee-line for the home trench I scrambled from crater to crater. So believe me when I tell you that I was astonished to run head-long into my old friend, Jim.

'You're alive! I'd given you up for dead. But quick, we can't talk here. There's a man out there who nearly got me killed and the Hun guns are rattling at a terrible pace'

Jim was expressionless. 'There's no-one out there.'

'Are you mad, just look behind...' but as I looked back there was nothing. The mist had risen and we were engulfed in a thick bank of fog. The noise had diminished to occasional crackles, harmless, like fireworks. 'But that's extraordinary; I swear there was someone out there. He was shouting after me, that's what started the guns off.' But it was like Jim wasn't really listening.

'Where do you think you're going, Harry?'

Jim still hadn't moved; he was eyeing me curiously.

'Why, back to the trenches, of course, where else?' I was starting to feel uneasy, something didn't feel right. This wasn't the Jim I knew. He moved forward a step and reached out to me, but I stumbled back and nearly fell.

'They'll kill you, Harry, you know that. You turned and ran, that's what they'll say.'

He had changed, I could see it more clearly now. The gleam in his eye had gone. The chattering man I knew had clammed up. I knew he was right, though, I couldn't return. I'd be shot as a traitor.

'But where can we go, if not back home?'

'We can survive out here. Look around, Harry. There's more ammunition than we could ever hope to use. There will be rations too, if we look.'

'But they're dead men's rations, Jim,' I was starting to feel cold, irritable, 'Where's the luck in scrounging around out here. What chance will we have?'

'This has never been a game of chance, Harry. This was always meant to be. We're bound to each other; don't you remember our pact? We promised to see each other through.'

Somehow, what he said made sense, but my doubts still niggled away. 'But there was someone out there, Jim. He was walking around, just like you and me. How can that be?'

'There are many things out here that you wouldn't expect, Harry. You must know that by now. You must know there's no going back; that we'll never return home. This is how we must exist. You can feel that, can't you?'

But I wasn't really listening. I was trying to remember about the figure in no-man's land. There was something familiar about him. Then it dawned on me.

'You remember you told me about the Frenchman you met when we first came out here, Jim? You remember the one, he told you about the sniper?'

Jim was nodding.

'I think there's some truth in that story. I think he might have been right. I saw him out there, I'm sure of it. Oh God, he saw me; does that mean he'll keep coming for me, they say he always gets his man. He walked through a fire fight like it was nothing. What are we going to do Jim, why don't you say something?'

Jim's expression had changed and I couldn't be sure if he was smirking, mocking me somehow. He asked me if the phantom had spoken.

'He did, you're right, he did say something. He said, take cover.'

'So he's not one of them then?'

'Not one of what?'

'He's not one of the enemy.'

'What are you talking about, man?' I'd started to pace; backwards and forwards, but enclosed in the mist I was too scared to walk far. I couldn't see more than five feet ahead.

Jim continued, 'If he spoke to you in English, then he probably isn't German. What uniform was he wearing, can you remember?'

'It wasn't a uniform exactly. He was wearing white sacking, streaked with oil; the type the snipers wear. That much I know.' I walked and tried to grab Jim, but he backed off, 'But I fear him. It's not natural the way he walked through no-man's land.'

'But you can't see him now, can you?'

Jim was looking north to enemy lines, as the haze started to lift, and I followed his gaze to try and find my man. It was dawn and the bright early morning light was casting a fresh light on the destruction. As the field started to warm under the sunshine the bluebottles arrived in numbers, with the ripe stench of the rotting flesh attracting legions of hungry insects. As I scanned the battlefield, the ground seemed to move, a heaving pulse of black, feasting on the memory of yesterday. I hadn't eaten for more than a day and my stomach churned as I tried to fight back the nausea.

When I stopped retching, I turned to find that Jim had vanished.

5

Far from danger, Charlie Balfour was alive and well.

I was struck down with dysentery a few days before the great offensive and was being treated in a field hospital for severe dehydration. The doctor told me that it was my own fault and that I should not have drank what I drunk. As if I had a choice in the matter! You see, fresh water's hard to come by and I'd filled up my canteen from a murky crater filled to the brim with rainwater. The doctor told me that I had chosen badly in the circumstances, and that I only had myself to blame. I'd taken him to task on that point, but when he asked me where my bowel movements took me when I got stuck in a pinch (if you get my drift) I finally realised what he was getting at.

And so it seems like I'm stuck here. I was glad too, make no mistake. It seemed as though we were close to something big. The heavy artillery had been blazing for days. The sound had been making me nervous, as if I wasn't on edge enough already. It was my pals, Jim and Harry, I felt bad for; I knew I might not see them again. I had been due to go on a recce through the lines with Jim, but my illness had given me a last minute reprieve, as so to speak. I suppose Jim will have already gone over the top and I haven't seen anything of Harry either. So much for the pals' battalion. But I knew dysentery wasn't something that would keep me out of action for long, so many of us had it. Oh to be back in Glasgow. I'd welcome the tension of a cup final over the lurch of my guts any day. I wonder if I'll ever see another game?

But it wasn't all bad, and it turned out that my misfortune was also my saving grace. I missed the Big Push on the first of July, and I took some comfort in knowing that I would never be one of the tens of thousands that died that day. It was merely delaying the inevitable, though, and I knew there would be many more days like it to come.

Officially we weren't being told much, but I knew from the casualties coming back through the hospital that it wasn't going to plan. They said they needed more space and I was moved back to a more intimate affair to recuperate. My nerves were in knots, though, as I felt certain that it wouldn't be long until I was called back into the fray.

In the end it was less than two weeks. I tried to delay my departure by complaining about the pain, but they wouldn't listen and I was sent on my way. Attached to the Royal Signals, communication is my line, and it's no easy task to lay cable under heavy fire. Worse still, with every fresh blast come new orders to review the network and fix the snags. I shuddered at the thought of having to risk life and limb in an exposed trench. You see, when a trench wall gets hit by an enemy shell you're forced to work out in the open. With no protection the Gerry snipers get a clear view, and I can tell you I've seen more than a few young boys that have stopped to gawk out into no-man's land for just a fraction of a second too long. That's all that it takes. They said the Somme would be over in days, but it's November now and there's no end in sight. The weather's starting to take a turn for the worse too, just my luck.

November 1916

On the morning of the 18th it started to snow and the attack began in sleet. After the long hot summer, the last few weeks had been wet, with large stretches of the trenches filling in quickly with flash floods. You try climbing out of a sticky clay death trap with thousands of gallons of water flooding in. I've seen a trench fill up in a matter of minutes and if you aren't quick off the mark, you get stuck fast in the mud. I've seen it happen more than once. When they get their feet bogged down there's not much to do but turn away. I mean, who wants to see that?

So, to recap, things were worse than usual, and I'd noticed that some of the boys had started talking about the sniper again, simply to pass the time.

It was a similar tale to the one I'd heard from Jim last year. The so-called Dead Eye phantom; firing-off in the depths of no-man's land. The one they said that never missed. But in time the story had changed, and it seemed the mysterious sniper was now taking all comers, regardless of allegiance. I listened at the mouth of the trench as two privates discussed the horror in earnest, and tried my best not to laugh as the bright eyed boys tried to scare themselves to death, as if they didn't have enough to worry about already.

'It's true. I've seen it with me own eyes.'

'Save yourself the trouble, man. I've heard all this before.'

'But it is true. A boy from Durham told me about it off the line.'

'Did it happen to a friend of his, eh? That's usually how it goes.'

'Don't laugh, mate. He told me he was out on a raid, looking to bring back some prisoners, when he saw the sniper, plain as day.'

'Way I heard, he only ever comes out at night.'

'So some say, but not this fella. He said the figure was dressed in a snipers' cowl. All bagged up, he was, with an Enfield rifle for company. His mate saw him first. The phantom was pointing his rifle at him, with his arms outstretched. He heard him say 'take cover,' over and over, all the time moving towards them. He told me that it wasn't long after that the firing started.'

'And I suppose when they looked back there was no-one there?'

Well I tell you what folks; it was about this time that I had heard just about enough.

As their field Sergeant I've a duty to maintain order, and the stories were getting out of hand. They're harmless enough at first, don't get me wrong, but as the daily grind continues and we're still launching attack after attack this kind of crap starts to get bad for morale. I stepped in with my big size tens to let them know the score.

'Listen, lads. There's nothing out there you need to fear apart from the Boche, and there's enough of them for all of us. They've stood firm against everything we've got, so we need every bit of guts going if we're going to press on and root them out. If we don't, then none of us will get to go home, and I doubt that's a thought that'll warm you through this nasty winter weather. So take heed lads, and cut out the chatter. Understood?'

The privates both nodded but I knew they weren't convinced. It was the weather doing the damage, slowing them down and making them fill the void with nonsense. Logic left them, and a fear of the elements crept in as a new enemy came to meet them, every bit as deadly as the soldiers over the way.

Out on the battlefield the many thousands of men who had fallen remained unclaimed. With no way to move them the flies had done their job and stripped the bodies bare, with skeletons strewn everywhere.

And there's more to come, I'm sure of that. I'd just taken receipt of orders that we'd be advancing on Boom Ravine come morning, to try and flush out the Germans. The stubborn bastards are dug-in deep up there; mark my words, with machine gun nests giving our boys an horrific welcome. Boom Ravine has earned its nickname and I'm in no hurry to give it another shot. What would Jim and Harry would make of all this?

Eventually, my mind drifted back to the talk of the sniper. It made me laugh what passed for entertainment in the trenches, especially the day before a push, when nerves were high and the boys were rattled. My good humour didn't last and tomorrow would be a day that lived long in my memory.

6

Time passed slowly for Jim West.

Sensations come and go but I feel like I'm swimming through treacle. I can't be sure of my position either. I've been scanning the horizon looking for signs of life, watching for patrols, but the waiting is interminable and I feel as if I've been in exile in no-man's land for years.

I could see that the lines were changing as land was won and lost. Progress came slowly, sometimes almost imperceptibly and by a matter of yards. Sometimes the victories were fleeting with the gains held for only a day or so, before the ground was retaken and the cycle began again. What remained a constant, though, was the threat of attack. I was struggling to make out their shapes in the murk and felt handicapped by the perpetual fog. But regardless of the conditions, I'm a marksman, and when I see a target I fire on sight. More often than not, once the shot rings out, the target falls. With an unlimited supply of scavenged ammunition it seemed I could stay out here forever, but at what cost and to what end? I wasn't sure anymore, but I felt compelled to continue my mission.

When winter finally came the conditions helped me to sharpen up. The crisp crunch of hardened snow meant I often heard the steps long before I saw my target. And with the dead carpeting the Somme valley, the crunch of bone underfoot pointed a path to the careless, when they ventured too close.

Through the murk of the freezing fog I spotted a group of eight men approaching. I tensed up as I got into position, preparing to take the shots from my 303 calibre Enfield rifle. With my body pressed down against the icy snow I felt nothing, with the task at hand consuming me completely. How many men had I shot? Hundreds, maybe thousands; I'd lost count. For months I'd stalked the trenches, watching as the patrols sloped across no man's land. It was clear that today's party were laying a new communications cable. The coiled wire unwound from the feeder as the line was laid to an abandoned trench about quarter of a mile from my position. It looked like a fresh attack was imminent.

I was partially hidden behind the remains of a tree trunk. Taking aim, I rotated the sights into focus as I picked out the man leading the patrol. The crosshairs marked him out, his time had come.

I pulled the trigger and he fell. The second and third men in the group looked around, they didn't know where I was, a mistake they wouldn't have long to consider. It was too late for them, though, and there was no margin for error. On the second shot the third man saw the flash but as he looked towards me his comrade fell; the blood arching back to earth from his jugular. The third man tried to run, but as he turned to make for the nearest crater my head shot hit home. The rest of the party needed no further warning and retreated back to safety.

'Good work, old man.'

It was Harry Lovett again. His visits seemed more frequent these days and his conversation was always the same, he wanted us to return to base.

'This is what I do now, Harry. There's no place for me back at base.'

Harry was admiring the rifle, which was still smoking from my latest success. 'You've got that down to an art form haven't you, Jim. I'll bet you're quite the legend back in the trenches. How do you feel about that?'

I shrugged off his questions and reloaded the rifle, 'As I said before, this is all I'm fit for.'

'You're wrong there, Jim. There's much more that you could be getting on with, much bigger things than this. You don't realise it yet, but you've done all you can. No-one will think any less of you, if you simply stop and move on.'

'No, it's you that doesn't understand. I've found my calling in this.'

Harry looked back hard, 'You have the gall to label this ritual slaughter as your calling. How far do you go before this consumes you completely, or is it already too late for that?'

'Why do you think we're here?' I was getting bored of these tiresome visits, and bored of Harry. We had been friends once, but he didn't have the nerve to carry on. He wasn't like me. I checked the barrel of the gun and clicked the first bullet into the chamber. Harry kept talking.

'Why are we here? That's a good question.' He was pointing at my rifle. 'I don't think that's the answer. I mean how does holding that thing even make you feel?'

I looked blankly ahead, hoping Harry would just give up and go. I've never been one to talk about my feelings. I knew he was right about one thing, though. I had lost my way, but there was nothing for it but to continue. I'd become numbed to dishing out death, and felt driven by a deep rooted duty and a divine right. I'd become a machine and I had no intention of stopping.

'It's too late for feelings, Harry.' These were words he needed to hear. 'You used to be able to help to me. You knew me once, but I just can't see the point in you anymore. All you want to do is leave. Well, I'm not stopping you, old pal. So feel free to go anytime the mood takes you.'

'But you can stop all this,' Harry swept his arm out across the battlefield, 'You can let it all go in a moment. If only you would look to yourself and accept the truth.'

'The truth, you sanctimonious bastard, is that I have no control. I am a sniper, and a good one too; one that's helping to win the war. And it's your war too, in case you'd forgotten. It seems that treachery's your way these days. I think you should go.'

'You can't even see what you're doing.'

'Look around you, Harry; I just wiped out a patrol. I helped to save lives.'

'You didn't even notice who you shot!'

'What are you on about, man?' I was getting tired of this but Harry kept talking.

'The last man you shot out there on patrol was Charlie. Our pal Charlie, who we swore to protect. He's the last of us and you didn't even blink when you fired.'

'Have you lost your mind?' I'd had enough and stood up toe-to-toe with my old friend, my anger rising as the mist grew thicker. It didn't faze Harry though, who couldn't help but chatter on.

'You didn't even recognise Charlie because you're too far gone. You'll never leave here Jim, it's become second nature and you can't even see it.'

I was trying to focus on what he was saying, but his words were fading. I looked back across to the position of the last patrol, but there was nothing there. The grey wall of frosted air hung heavy on the fields of the Somme, but there was not a living soul in sight. In the distance a whizz bang broke the silence, as shells arched towards the allied trenches. I fell back into position and waited. Harry could go to hell.

The bullet ricocheted off his helmet and Charlie Balfour fell to the ground.

Hit by the sniper I lay wheezing in the muddy crater that had saved my life. Its frozen peaks and the splintered shards of shrapnel I'd landed on cut through my uniform and dug deep into my flesh. The sniper had finished off two of us, while the others had left me for dead. I can't say that I blamed them. I'd have done the same in their shoes.

The past few weeks had thrown up too many surprises and I longed for the days when I could soldier with certainty. The early promise of the first offensive had dwindled away when it became clear that the Germans were in it for the long haul. Time and time again we battered their lines and they kept bouncing back. It seemed there was nothing they couldn't take. Now they were using the terrain against us, with snipers and machine gun posts dug into craters, masked with tarpaulin, invisible until it was too late. Four of us had died in the last week alone. But in this weather, in these temperatures; you had to hand it to the Germans – these lads had stamina.

And then today I'd finally come face-to-face with the mysterious sniper. The young boys called him Dead Eye; he'd taken on the mantle of the phantom the French had yakked on about all those months ago. But this chap seemed indiscriminate in his targets. He was known as a soldier gone mad; living the life of a lone wolf in no man's land. I knew he had to be stopped, but it wouldn't be by me.

Although I hadn't made my objective, the communications cable still fed back an open channel to HQ. Frigid with cold, my shaking hands struggled clumsily to wire up the field telephone. The sniper had got it wrong today, and it was going to prove a costly mistake. I called in a couple of surprise packages and couldn't resist a smile when I saw his nest ripped apart as our shells hit home.

'How do you like that, you bastard?'

Quietly, I slipped back to the front line. As far as I was concerned, the sniper was dead. It wasn't long before I re-joined my battalion. We were back out on patrol just two days later.

7

For 150 years the red shutters welcomed visitors to the steading, with the land around it among the most productive in the Somme. The Bertillon clan had set out to create a modest family business in 1765, and through generations of dedication and hard work they had transformed their land into a notable success. But their fortune turned on the spin of a Franc and one day, not two years ago, the building was abandoned as the war encroached on this once peaceful retreat.

Today, it lay in ruins. The latticed props which once held the pitched roof were exposed from blast damage; its front side blown out. Charlie Balfour was eyeing the building from around a quarter of a mile away. Squinting through his field glasses, it looked like the contents of the building had been vomited out onto the courtyard. But there was no sign of activity which made it the perfect place to set up camp for the night. They'd all be thankful for the shelter.

Looking around inside, I could see the place had been badly bombed. Massive sections of the ground floor had been obliterated, with splintered floorboards hanging down into the basement like thorny stalactites. But the concealed lower floor was an added extra that offered protection from incoming shells.

Lighting a small fire, the black fumes quickly filled the basement and filtered out through the holes in the floor above. It wasn't ideal, but it was tolerable, and better than digging down into a new trench or bivouacking in some half-filled crump hole.

Today had been a good day, with only two badly injured and no dead. Fighting was a problem, though, as the rules had changed, and no-one knew what to expect. I was getting jittery and trying to hide my nerves. We'd been tasked with laying a cable through to a position that had been, until recently, well behind the German front line. The trouble being that no-one seemed to have a clue about where the enemy had gone. Spread out and fighting from crater to crater, the old defensive lines had all but disappeared. Every fresh step into the unknown brought the threat of hidden danger. The new German storm troopers were establishing a fierce reputation, and when you saw the black masked uniforms of the flame thrower divisions, stalking through the battlefield with fire scorching everything in its path, you pretty much wanted to turn and run. But that wasn't an option. HQ said they needed more forward information; claimed the Germans were getting too much on us without us knowing who was giving it up. It was making everyone twitchy, and being stuck out here in the middle of nowhere wasn't a good place to settle your nerves. But we made do; so I kipped down and waited for my turn on watch.

***

It was at about 03:00 hours that I heard the first shot. From the old kitchen I had a pretty good view of the German sections, but the gunfire came from the other direction, from back the way we came. I thought it might be a raid and decided to investigate. I knew what I'd rather do, but I had my orders. There's another shot; not far distant. Damn, this isn't good. There was a staircase in the hall which was badly damaged but still passable. Looking up I saw there was a grand bay window on the first floor landing that would provide a much better vantage point of the landscape to the rear so I decided to climb up. Where the steps disappeared I used the steel runners which held the structure in place to tip-toe up three feet, hanging on to the mangled bannister for support. Eventually, though, I made the position and peered out looking for signs of life.

Fifteen minutes later I'd heard nothing more and I wondered if I might have overreacted. Then, off in the distance, I heard the crack of a single shot and saw a pin prick of light; the unmistakable flare of an Enfield rifle. One of our snipers was busy, but it's a fool that shoots at night. Even I knew the light would give him away; he stood little to no chance of taking another shot without being seen. It was suicide.

It goes without saying that my curiosity held my interest. I was intrigued as to what might happen next. In earlier days, on occasions like these, we took bets on how long it would be before the shooting stopped, but with so many of us now dead, the sport had lost its sheen.

It had been pitch black until that point and then the cloud lifted, allowing the strong light of the hunter's moon to blaze its path over the battlefield. I could see the snow was beginning to melt, and the shabby remains of the fallen were starting to emerge from their frozen tombs. Rusted guns, flasks and helmets lay bundled up in shredded khaki, while the bones of thousands more remained unknown and unclaimed.

The flicker of movement caught my eye about a mile off to the south. I could see four figures, hunched low, and carrying something heavy. It looked like a German machine gun crew looking for a new position, although I couldn't be certain.

Their moonlighting was interrupted when the firing began. One man flopped over; he didn't know what had hit him. I scanned the horizon to try and see where the next shot would come from. The light was nearer to me than I first thought; no more than 100 yards. I fixed the position in my head and made my way back downstairs. Out the door and across the field I ran as fast as I dared and looked for the patrol. In the stark light night I saw that one man still stood, perhaps the sniper was reloading. I was running faster now, pistol in hand and ready to help if I could. The final flash meant the last of the Boche was down. I was close now, with just yards to go.

But when I made his position, there was no-one there, just the remnants of an abandoned firing platform. I could see that a low wall of sandbags had been demolished by heavy machine gun fire. On closer inspection there were human remains; another sniper lay unmolested but very dead. He lay outstretched with rifle in hand, with his helmet down over his face, and camouflage sacking in place. Bending down I lifted the metal visor, pinching the rim between my thumb and forefinger. But beneath, there was nothing but skull and bone. This sniper had been here for some time. I started to worry that I might have walked into a trap and cursed myself for not stopping to think.

I needed to leave and decided that attack would be the best form of defence. From memory I knew roughly where the patrol had been and made my way the half mile or so to their position, using the backdrop of my garret to plot the course. Perhaps the sniper had gone across to make sure he had finished the job. His support could prove to be my saving grace.

The former farmland had seen heavy action and the rough ground made for slow going as I stumbled through the slush and muck. In the end I didn't so much find the patrol as fall into it. The four men had fallen back into a crater. Their MG08 machine gun was lodged, barrel down, in the mud, while the soldiers lay strewn across the crater. But what I saw made no sense as the crump hole was ripe with the stench of decaying flesh and the screech of sated rats. I couldn't understand it. I'd seen these men shot not an hour ago, but the patrol was in the same state as the sniper. They'd all been dead for at least a month.

I was gripped by a sudden panic, as my straining eyes seemed to betray my common sense. Had I been fighting for so long that I was now plagued by visions like those I'd mocked in my own men. But the sniper had been real. I'd heard the shots. I'd seen the patrol dispatched. Now, looking at the evidence with my own eyes – but what am I saying? This is ridiculous; it can't be the same group. Think, Charlie, think. You've got lost at night and your co-ordinates are wrong.

Convinced of my mistake I left the crater to look for the real targets and was confronted by the man I'd been looking for from the start. Thank God. I thought I'd gone quite mad! I laughed out loud when I realised that I'd been shaking at the thought of being pursued by phantoms, when all along I'd simply taken a wrong turn. The sniper was standing right in front of me, not less than forty yards away. He held his Enfield in one arm and his ammunition bag in the other. He was an imposing figure and seemed to glow under the bright moonlight. In the background I could hear the rap of pistols, as a skirmish broke out; how far away was difficult to say, but close enough to mean trouble.

'Get down man,' I hissed, 'you're a sitting target.'

But the sniper didn't move. His face was masked by his unnerving camouflage, his shape distorted by the baggy sacking designed to disguise his presence to foes in the field.

'Damnit man, can't you hear me?' I'd crouched down, convinced the patrol must still be around somewhere, 'Get down, won't you, or we'll both be killed.'

But he didn't seem to care and I was amazed when instead of blending back into the landscape as his profession demanded, the sniper raised his arm and pointed back towards my garret. He stood there for what seemed like an age. When he spoke, his voice was strangely distorted.

'TAKE COVER.'

'What,' I said, barely able to hear the whisper.

'TAKE COVER, CHARLIE BALFOUR. TAKE COVER, OR DIE.'

I was dumbstruck that he knew my name and while I was sure that we hadn't met, there was something familiar in the sniper's way that I couldn't put my finger on. While I tried to remember where I might know him from, my thoughts were interrupted by the familiar sound of an incoming whizz bang. Looking east I saw the shell approaching. I ran at full pelt, stumbled and dived for cover in a crater. Four shells came in quick succession and I knew I'd been foolish to stand exposed like that for so long.

The ordnance had come close and the enemy would probably think I'd been hit, so I decided to stay put until it was safe to leave. But a short while later I heard firing back at the farmhouse and crept out of the crater and made my way back to base, to lend a hand with the counter attack if help were needed.

The sniper was no-where to be seen.

8

To say that I was surprised not to walk into a fire fight back at the farmhouse is an understatement. In fact there were no signs of trouble at all, which was more than a little confusing. When I first arrived back I'd asked what all the shooting was about but they all said the same thing; that it had been quiet all night. They had seemed more concerned about me. I argued my piece but no-one could vouch for my strange encounter. I backed down when I saw the worried glances being cast around the basement and told them I was tired. I took to mulling it over from the comfort of a chair I'd found upended in the debris.

The sniper had been real and the more I thought about it the more I was sure that I had heard the voice before, although it seemed impossible. It had been Jim West out there. Now, I know how that sounds. It's an admission that will likely make you question my sanity. I knew that Jim was dead; he could well have been one of the first to have been lost in the Big Push, back in July. I'll admit to you that his voice had changed some, with his rasping delivery disguising his identity. Even so, I was certain that it was him; it was more than just a feeling. Listen to me rambling on. Could that really have been Jim? In my heart I knew my friend had been dead for months, but coming face-to-face with the sniper out in the field, I sensed a bond, almost like I was reconnecting with something, like I could feel his spirit.

I sighed and wished for leave, even just a day would give me time to think this through. I've seen too much and my mind is on edge. But I'm not mad, no way – I can't be. I've seen it happen to others and I won't let it take me. They won't brand me a coward.

I pulled myself together. I knew that whoever it was that I'd seen, it could not have been Jim. No-one could survive in no man's land through the winter; not even Jim West.

***

Activity at the front tailed off for a spell, and rumours suggested that this was the calm before the storm; that the Germans might finally be preparing for a major offensive. I didn't think that likely.

Although they'd been stubborn in their defence, they'd made no real effort to strike out for territorial gains. All the same, maybe the gossips were onto something this time. It was certainly true that there had been little action to speak of in the last few days. I've seen next to nothing save for the occasional sharpshooter. It seems that everything boils down to those bloody snipers.

The break in the fighting and the ensuing thaw gave us the time we needed to harvest the dead. Countless thousands of bodies had lain for weeks, with artillery blasting the bones carelessly across the mud. Looking out across the miles of wasteland it seemed unlikely that many could have survived intact, but there were many who could still be buried and that would surely be good for morale.

Circumstances presented me with an opportunity and I was temporarily seconded to the Corps Burial Officers, which had been commissioned to identify and reclaim the dead. I managed to wangle a posting near Albert, back where it all began. I knew this might be the only chance I would get to find out for sure. I needed to know, beyond a reasonable doubt, that my friends had been laid to rest.

***

Standing on the original line it was hard to look out over the blackened ruin of what had once been productive farmland. I laughed thinking back to the gentlemen's agreement between the French and Germans and their six shells a day. It seemed so ridiculously quaint. So much had happened since then. Of the old Tram Battalion, I'd lost count of how many had died and I stopped trying to find out. I found that it was easier simply to exist.

My time off the line, or in tactical, was the easiest. The only constant on those days was a fear of losing my tobacco, and armed with my smokes I coped as best I could. Drawing deeply on the crumpled fag my thoughts wandered back to the old days in Glasgow with Jim and Harry. Losing them had been hard. Getting killed hadn't been something that had even entered our minds when we'd rushed to enlist. We were young and our sense of life outweighed any real appreciation of death. So we made a pact to see each other through the war, come thick or thin. It seemed like a lifetime had passed since then. I took another draw on my fag, trying to kindle the last strands of tobacco and find an ember of comfort in the heat. But my fingers got burnt on the glowing end, so I flicked the offending article over the top of the trench in disgust. For all our good intentions, it didn't seem friendship counted for much out here after all. For the sake of my memories, I swore on my life that I would do everything I could to make things right.

**

The salvage operation was already in full swing when I arrived. The Lieutenant co-ordinating my section told me that a book of the dead was being compiled and with each new body came a fresh entry. Where we could we used the identification tags to put a name to a man, but for those with none, the soldiers were buried five or six at a time. Leafing through the fast expanding tome was a dispiriting experience, with name after name telling the same depressing story. After about ten minutes I found one of the names I had hoped to find:

Pvt Harry Lovett, Highland Light Infantry, 15th Battalion (Died – Albert, Somme, 1916)

It took my breath away at first. Seeing the name written down like that was like taking a shot to the side. As the unwelcome flood of reality washed away my defences, I couldn't stop from sobbing.

Years later I'd find out that Harry had barely made it out of the trenches. He had gone over as part of the second wave and had been clipped by shrapnel, badly cutting himself. He'd been trying to stem the flow of blood from the wound when he was taken out by God knows who. He should have been looking ahead, rather than trying to sort himself out. He'd always been the practical one of the group, always had an idea to sort things out. Not this time though. At home they said he'd died a heroes' death, but I don't even know what that means.

**

I spent the rest of the day in the mud, dragging the remains of soldiers from the tight grasp of the clay which had been blighting our efforts for months. Many of the men were little more than skeletons, held together like bags of bones in their slowly rotting uniforms. They all had one thing in common; none of them were Jim West. I salvaged, logged and returned the boys I could, back to the waiting area. They'd all be buried somewhere, but they were no longer my concern, and my search continued.

***

That night I returned to the old front line alone, guided by the light of a full moon. Having helped lay the communications cable ahead of the first attack, I knew roughly where Jim would have been stationed. But with few remaining landmarks, I didn't have high hopes of tracking him down.

The ground had changed a lot since the start of the offensive. The Somme's godforsaken terrain had been continually churned up, and the waves of abandoned trenches made walking freely across the wasteland a tricky affair. Weaving through the countless lost I checked tags where I could, and did my best to avoid getting bogged down myself. If I got stuck, there would be no-one around to drag me out, a self-inflicted wound. And so I travelled with care. But at one in the morning, despite my best efforts, my world collapsed.

9

The change was subtle at first, then it all seemed to happen quite quickly. With a low mist hugging the ground, an uneven glow blanketed a wasteland punctured by the peaks of craters and the splintered tree trunks which rose above the murk. The ground was treacherous enough in daylight, doubly so under heavy fire, and as the fog spread I could see nothing underfoot and was at the mercy of my own surefootedness. I took a deep breath and hoped for a measure of good luck.

Moonlight can do strange things to a man's eyes and I was not sure if my long war and current state of mind were starting to pay a heavy toll on my senses. In the background I could see an army on the move. Shapes emerged from the fog as the ghostly forms of fallen soldiers charged silently through the night. There were too many to count. Some walked slowly with bayonets thrust forward, while others ran swiftly past. The blank stares in their eyes told their own story. For there was no hope for any of these men – no rest to be had in the army of the dead. I had barely moved when the noise started to bleed through and the silence was shattered.

The sounds they made. The wails of men left to die in a perpetual agony. One of them was almost close enough to touch as he drifted past. The soldier presented a terrible sight. His jaw had been blown off, but he kept on walking, gun pointed forward. I could see that he was aware of what was happening and that he saw me too. He gave off an odd sideways look, as if he were begging for help, but was compelled to continue.

It was then that I realised that I'd made a fundamental mistake; the phantoms weren't acting out an attack but fleeing; running from a looming figure in white who blasted fierce salvos from an Enfield rifle. A single bullet from the old lines cut through the ghost battalion like a tracer bullet, with the army decimated in seconds.

For all I had seen these last two years, my fear was absolute. I felt that I may have tipped over the edge, but all the while this felt so real. I couldn't look away. With each fresh contact the bullets extinguished the apparitions in its path, with the form of the dead dissolving back in the fugue below. I knew instinctively that the figure was coming for me. We'd met so many times before and it seemed this was finally the end. Jim West was standing with gun in hand, firing from the hip, his blank stare directed squarely at me.

'TAKE COVER,' he said. 'TAKE COVER, CHARLIE BALFOUR.'

But I wasn't ready. I'd come here to save him, 'No, Jim. This is not your way. This is not what we were. We were friends Jim, the best of friends.' I ran forward, not caring if I tripped or fell. I needed to make contact with my friend to try and break the spell which held him on the Somme. As I drew nearer, Jim took aim. We were alone now, the phantom army vanquished back to earth. I eyed the barrel from not fifteen feet, almost close enough to touch him, when he fired.

'TAKE COVER, OR DIE,' again the grizzled warning poured forth.

Certain my end had come I felt my feet fall from beneath me and I slipped away.

When I awoke it was morning. There was a hard frost beneath me but the sun was strong and had already begun to warm the earth. I could taste blood in my mouth and realised I must have landed badly and injured myself. Sitting up I realised that I must have fallen into what had once been a trench. In the roughly cut walls were the bodies of men that had been buried alive. Left to their makeshift graves, they'd been uncovered as fresh trenches were dug and their bodies ignored, as new burrows were furrowed in the name of fleeting progress.

Addiction gnawed at me and I struck a light and smoked my first fag of the day. It tasted acrid after my fall, but what exactly had happened? Had I been dreaming after all? I knew I would have to get back. I wasn't sure how long I'd been out of commission but the risk of court martial increased for every moment I remained unaccounted for. Trying to think of a way to save myself, I thought I might still make roll call if I moved fast.

There were wooden steps part way down the trench and as I strode down to leave I kicked at a Brodie helmet that had been left discarded in the mud. It didn't budge and there was a sickening crack when the metal nudged at something below but didn't move. Now I'd been around for long enough to realise the risk of booby traps, but I felt compelled to lift the helmet to see what lay beneath.

I don't mind telling you that it was as sad a sight as I ever saw, with a soldier buried face down with tufts of hair sticking up through the mud. The trench had obviously been well used at one time and soldiers had been busy on patrol, with a bald patch having been worn down into the back of this poor man's head by the passage of men in a hurry. They'd placed the helmet there to act as a spring board. What a way to go.

I scraped back some of the earth to reveal the top of his uniform. Turning back his collar, I saw the man's name stitched on the inside. I felt a surge of adrenalin which brought a rush of blood to my cheeks. I started to dig furiously at the sides of the head. Encased in mud, the body was still relatively well preserved and when I had gone down a couple of inches I was able to find purchase under his shoulder blades and pull him up and over, releasing him from his shallow grave. I turned him on his side to be met with a familiar sight. Jim West had a bullet through his temple. Last night hadn't been a vision after all. Jim had known I was coming for him.

I sat there for what seemed like an age with his lifeless head cradled in my lap.

***

My reverie was broken when a voice boomed out over the lip of the trench.

'What have we got here then, thought it was time for a nap did we?' If this was the end of me then I was ready to leave. 'No rest for the wicked, son. Up and at 'em. We've got work to do.'

The salvage team was already in action and they were kind enough to let me work on that day with no questions asked. That day my old friend, Jim West, was the first to be returned to the massed graves that were starting to take shape off the line.

They said I'd been lucky to find him.

10

I stayed lucky and lasted the war. They said I was lucky anyway, called me a hero when I got home. I'd fought through the Somme, Arras, Ypres, and through the 100 days offensive. They gave me a Victoria Cross for my troubles, but what did that matter now? I felt old and tired but at 21 my life was only just beginning. Back home the older ones all wanted to buy me a drink. They were keen to hear the details.

'What was it like? Did you kill anyone? Did you give the Kaiser a good kick up the arse, son?'

Life was supposed to return to normal, but the things I'd seen wouldn't leave me and I found it difficult to settle back into my old routine. The respect of my friends and family was well intentioned, but it still felt misplaced when measured against the blood soaked reality of trench warfare. I was expected to forget the war and move on, but I couldn't, so I drank. At night the pubs were half as busy as they had been before the war, but twice as loud, as empty men sought refuge in the bottle.

If the war had taught me anything it was how to survive, so I pulled on my civvies and went back to drive the trams. Through Cathcart and into town I went round in circles, day after day, always ending back at the same place.

In time, a memorial went up at the depot for all the men that had died from the old Tram Battalion. That life seemed like a dream, now. I couldn't even remember what half of them looked like, and we never talked about them; the wounds were still too raw.

It pains me to admit it, but I always think of Jim lying forgotten in a deserted trench. He comes to me in dreams. His ghostly figure points and he asks me to lay him to rest. But I'd done that already, so what can he want of me now? I've done all I can for Jim and Harry, so why does it still feel so bloody hard to live with?

***

There were many nights that I stayed back at the depot and stared at the memorial. It was a huge dark wood affair with ornate edging and the insignia of the Highland Light Infantry.

'In proud and affectionate remembrance of their supreme sacrifice.' I read it out loud, repeating the names again and again, trying to remember but always skipping over the two that I never really wanted to acknowledge. For hours I would sit, trying to think about what I could have done differently to help save their lives. Perhaps, if I'd gone out over the top on the first of July I could have done something for Harry. But it was a useless thought to entertain. It would have been just as likely that I'd be dead too. Even so, the guilt weighed heavily. I couldn't let it go. It wasn't just me back from the war but none of us wanted to talk about it and, in time, the others stopped asking. All of us that were there remembered what had happened. We all jumped when there were loud bangs in the repairs yard, as our minds snapped back to our personal wars. This living hell was something we were all haunted by, even though for many of us, it had been freely chosen.

As the years went on, I saw Jim and Harry more and more. Sometimes I'd pick out a face on the street and call them out, only to find a stranger; and it was always someone else because you can't cheat time.

And that was my life. Consumed with guilt and with no zest to start again, time dragged on at a snail's pace, with every day the same. I sought refuge in the city's worst pubs. I loved when I could and fought at every given opportunity. They used to be scared of me, a veteran of the Great War, but I knew I could barely defend myself these days. I worked for pay day and the beer flowed freely every Friday. For a couple of hours my ghosts were forgotten. The jokes and the banter staved off my nightmares, if only for a short while.

July 1st, 1933

One night, about 15 years after the war ended, I stumbled out of Samson's bar and was weaving my way back home. It was a misty night and the moon shone down brightly to light up the department store windows at the corner of Buchanan and Argyle Street. In the distance I heard the last tram of the day rattle its way down the street; hot on my heels. I'd been following the steel tracks, trying to walk in a straight line.

A few moments later and much closer now, I heard the rumble of the approaching car and a voice cried out for me to take cover. The words hit home hard as memories blazed through my mind. The warning shook me with such force that I felt sober in a split second, amazed to be facing my oldest nightmare once more.

'TAKE COVER,' repeated the voice, this time the cry had become a shrill scream.

Peering into the gloom of that foggy night in Glasgow I was suddenly blinded by a bright light, while the smell of decay overwhelmed me.

'TAKE COVER, OR DIE,' the voice screamed. The tram's brakes screeched as the driver tried in vain to slow down.

I twisted round, eyes ablaze with fear to see the sniper once more. It was then that it dawned on me that I'd been wrong all these years. Jim West didn't want to be found; he'd been angry that I'd survived.

I fell back, desperate to escape the piercing bullet. But it was too late; my luck had run out. He would not be denied again.

My body lay under the wheels of the tram. A small crowd had gathered to watch, wondering if I was dead or alive. Then, in the distance I heard the drone of battle as bullets buzzed like bees all around me. It was as if I'd never left.

I looked up and saw Jim West side-by-side with Harry Lovett, both of them glowing like torches in the night. I remembered then that as friends we had always promised to see each other through the war. I hadn't been true to my word.

My long lost friends leaned in to welcome me back to the fold and I was cast back to a ruined landscape that had seared itself onto my consciousness. As the present fades I embrace the past and take my place in the pockmarked battlefields of the Somme.

The Rocking Stone

The Rocking Stone

In Threepwood lies the Lady,
by the circle of the Rocking Stone.
Her warning comes from ages past,
cast out from the otherworld.

If you come to see her once, take heed,
she won't be far from home.
She shall not stop, she'll seek you out,
from the fire of the Rocking Stone.

Anon

1

Threepwood, 1983

If we could remember all the stories that define a lifetime, would we still have a sense of who we really are? I thought I knew, once, but looking back I'm not so sure. I used to view the world with certainty, but I've seen and done things that have eroded my morals to little more than a survival instinct. If my younger self had known what the future held perhaps my life would have been different. But that's not possible now; and worse than that, history is about to repeat itself.

In the beginning I thought the Lady of Threepwood was nothing more than a story, a childish fantasy and a fragment of my past. But it's more than that. Ultimately it's all I've ever known.

Drawn from black dust cast out from the otherworld the legend ran that the Lady of Threepwood sought death. Worshipped by the druids as a God like figure, they said the spectre had been trapped by a curse and would not stop until her debt was repaid, the circle complete.

And here I am, back at the Rocking Stone for the final time; prepared to face the reckoning. It had been my own words that had compelled me to return. Wrenched from the sodden earth, the ritual brought me back, first as just a glimpse; then whipped up from dust to face my true form once more. From the stone perimeter, I saw flames engulfing the land around the Rocking Stone. As the chant continued, the flames rose higher and I moved towards the centre.

Vengeance will soon be mine.

Peggy Balfour, Threepwood, 1953

I remember the night well. I was ten years old and I'd been sitting, huddled together with my mother on a threadbare red settee, with only the glowing hearth to heat us through the cold winter evening. It was the perfect time for tales of the 'otherworld', as she liked to call them. Father said they were 'an affront to the Almighty', but one thing was sure – the women of the house were both fond of stories, and of one in particular.

'Tell me again, mother.' I looked up, smiling, trying to work out if she was in the mood to let me stay up late. It was difficult to make out her features in the gloom, with the flickering light from the fire casting orange embers past her eyes.

'Oh, Peggy, not again – how many times can I tell it?' She was shifting in her seat. It was past my bedtime, but I knew she'd continue if I pressed a little longer. She was already showing signs of relenting, 'You must know it off by heart?' My mother was making a great effort to look hard done by, but I knew from her look that she'd already made up her mind.

'Just once more; please, mother?' I kept up my side of the performance and cuddled-in more closely, making sure to beg with the eyes she said looked like moonbeams.

Ann Balfour sighed. 'Well, OK, but we'll need to be quick.' She was trying to sound harassed, but the gleam in her eye told another story, 'It's getting late and there's work to do in the morning.'

I smiled and agreed, 'Start with the rhyme.'

The wind was fierce outside and a gust barrelled down the chimney and stoked the fire. The last piece of charred wood awoke from its slumber and flickered back to life; it seemed like the perfect moment.

'You're daft on that rhyme aren't you, girl? I'll tell it to you one more time but as I always say, remember it's all just a story.'

We were sitting closely together, and I found the heat from her body comforting, 'Start with the rhyme,' I whispered, anxious that we should begin in case she changed her mind and sent me to bed. I watched as my mother composed herself, preparing to scare me to death with her favourite story. When she spoke, it was in a low voice, which I had to strain to hear.

'In Threepwood lies the Lady, by the circle of the Rocking Stone. Her warning comes from ages past, cast out from the otherworld. If you come to see her once, take heed, she won't be far from home. She shall not stop, she'll seek you out...'

She paused, as she always did, for dramatic effect, and even though I knew what to expect, I jumped when the last line came roaring from her tiny frame, 'From the fire of the Rocking Stone.' The tension broke and we both laughed as she lunged forward and tickled my ribs until it hurt. In the hearth the log was now well aflame. I could feel the warmth creep back into the room. I laughed so much my face was wet with tears. Eventually, I composed myself enough to ask the one question I'd never yet got a satisfactory answer to. 'But who was the lady?'

Mother looked at me with her serious face. It always seemed she knew more about the story than she let on, but so far she'd refused to tell me more, 'No-one really knows, Peggy, but the story's been around for centuries. Some say she was a druid, cursed to walk the hills until she was avenged for the wrongs that had been done to her.'

Druids had always interested me. Our farm was about three miles from the nearest town, and sat off a single track road which ran through Threepwood. The land was hilly and thick with bog. I'd asked Joe Meek about it once; he'd worked on the farm since mother was my age. He said that anyone who'd tried to grow crops had failed on account of the land being no good. It was hard for me to believe but Joe insisted that Threepwood had once been lush forest and that's why the druids had come here. Joe's so serious all the time, he makes me laugh.

I knew a fair bit about our land too. On the top of Cuff Hill, which towers above our farm, the Rocking Stone sits in the centre of a stone circle, with birch trees around the perimeter. Joe told me that it had been a spot where the druids made sacrifices. Not far off were four small standing stones. Joe said the ancient order had used them for terrible rituals, that they didn't know right from wrong and that they knew no sin. I didn't know how that would be possible. The local minister was quick to tell us when we were doing anything wrong, even if it seemed like nothing. Father said he had an opinion on everything. But it seemed it hadn't always been that way. Joe said that if you were picked for a druid sacrifice it was seen as an honour. He said they made no distinction between being dead and alive, with all things mixed up in a sort of 'cosmic soup', whatever that meant.

And then there was the Lady of Threepwood. I'd often heard the tales of people having seen the woman in white who supposedly stalked Cuff Hill. They said she only ever appeared if someone was about to die. My mother said she'd seen the woman more than once, not long before Grandpa died. I didn't know if that was just another of her stories. All I knew was that despite years of looking I'd never even caught a glimpse. Back in front of the fire, I came out of my dream and looked back to my mother.

'Tell me about the day they found the druids' graves.' She didn't like this bit as much and I noticed that she'd often try to change the subject. She moved off the settee to put another log on the fire, lingering longer than normal as she watched the smoke wisp from the log before bursting into flames. I don't know how long I'd been watching, but when she turned around she jumped back, knocking a cup from the mantle, which shattered on the granite floor, breaking the silence.

'My goodness, child, you gave me quite a fright.'

She was trying to change the subject again. 'Why do you never like talking about the graves?'

My mother shifted uneasily, picking at her teeth with her thumbnail, 'It's not that I don't like talking about it, it's that even after all these years I don't really know what happened.'

'It was when they built the new road wasn't it?'

Ann Balfour, 1933

I was 13 then and the new road through Threepwood had been a big event in all our lives. It had been a sweltering summer's afternoon and I'd watched from the farmhouse as the workmen shattered rock and shifted earth to lay the parish road from Beith. It had been little more than a dirt track before, and with more motor cars on the road the Council said that 'progress' was required. And what a sight; the large smoking machines were like something from a dream. Like it or not, I knew my landscape was changing. In the distance I noticed that work had stopped and I walked around the reservoir at the foot of the hill and closer to the site of the road to get a better look. There were more workers than usual, with cloth caps being wrung in a sea of fat, muscled hands. The machines fell silent.

As I got nearer I sensed that they'd found something unusual. A tall man was shaking his head as he addressed the rest of the crew.

'We can't go through this. Someone will need to go into town and telephone the Council.'

As I watched, peeking out from behind a birch tree, a small squat man started speaking, apparently unimpressed, 'Ach Billy, let's just move it,' he said, 'this is all just rubble and dust.'

Billy wasn't convinced. He shook his head again and pointed to a large flat stone which had been uncovered about ten feet away, 'We can't just destroy it. There's something inside. It looks like some kind of box.'

Creeping closer I could see what he meant. The men had unearthed what looked like a hidden grave. There were four thin stone wedges propping up a fifth which formed a lid to ground level. One side of the grave had been split by the road works, and inside was an ancient looking metal box. 'What's that, Mister?' I asked. They all seemed surprised to see me, apparently unaware I'd been watching all this time.

'Where have you come from, lass?' I pointed backwards across the water to the farm, 'I live over there.'

'Do you have a telephone? It would save us a trip.' I shook my head. In all my 13 years I'd never even seen a telephone, let alone used one. At any rate, the question seemed a distraction, and I wanted to know more.

'Is it a grave?'

Billy looked down at me. He seemed a little irritated, and was short in his response, 'We don't know what it is.'

'Do you think there are clues inside, like in the mystery books?'

'Ffft.' He'd lost interest in me and turned back to the crew, 'For now lads, the work is over. Come back tomorrow and we'll see how we're set.' I heard murmurings of a visit to the Saracen's Head, where my father went for meetings, and watched as the group collected their things and walked off, disappearing over the brow of the hill a short while later, as they made their way down the valley and back to town. Before long just the tall man, Billy, remained.

'Why haven't you gone, too?' I asked, 'Are you the boss?'

He laughed as he bent down and looked me in the eye, 'Full of questions, aren't you? I'll bet you don't get much excitement up here, do you?'

I didn't know what he meant. My father said the farm kept us all busy; that we didn't want for more and knew no different. And that had always been true; up until now, anyway.

'Well, you're a strange one, that's for sure.' He was watching me closely. Maybe he thought I was going to say something else. I didn't understand what he wanted and stayed quiet for a moment. Billy nodded and gestured for me to follow him, 'Since you're so nosey, maybe we can have a closer look inside. I promise not to tell anyone if you won't?'

I returned his smile and watched as Billy reached inside the grave and started to drag out the box, the metal scraping off the rocks. It seemed heavy and it took about ten minutes to break it free. Eventually, Billy laid it on top of the flat rock and stood back to take a closer look. The black box was made of a heavy metal which was warped and rusted with age. The box was bound by three black bands which had strange symbols on the clasps. Billy swore loudly as he struggled to prise it open.

'By God, I don't know how long this thing's been here, but it doesn't look like it's going to give up its secrets today.' He nodded off into the distance, something had caught his eye, 'Anyway, it looks like your mother's here to take you home, and not before time.'

But I knew my mother had gone to town. She wasn't due back until late that night. There was only me and Joe at the farm today, and he was out on the hills. When I turned I saw a woman in white flowing robes standing not far off. She seemed familiar, but I couldn't clearly see her face.

'That's not my mother,' I said to Billy, 'I don't know who that is.'

It all happened so fast. A strong gust of wind appeared from nowhere, knocking me back and taking my breath away. The box burst open and thick black ash covered me. I choked on the soot which had me gagging for air. Tears streaked down my face as I tried in vain to take a breath. Then came release. I felt my back being slapped hard and a voice telling me to breathe. But the pain was only making it worse and I could feel my cheeks burn as I gasped for air. With one retching cough the blockage cleared and the cool fresh air restored me to life. The woman in white had vanished.

I never saw Billy again. I didn't find out for several days but I overhead my mother saying that he'd collapsed and died. She said he'd had a heart attack, that he must have been worried sick that he'd been responsible for what had happened to me. After that, things were never the same again.

2

After the incident at what they were calling the druids' graves, everyone agreed that I'd suffered 'a shock' and the doctor told me to take a complete break for the next seven days. Freed from the treadmill of chores and school I'd never had so much spare time and to my delight I found that filling my day was easy. A large part of the back wall of our sitting room had been given over to rows and rows of dusty old books. Gathered through the decades, the library was something my parents were proud of. Education was important to them; they said that farming was changing, and I'd been encouraged to open my eyes to as many different ideas as possible. Scanning the shelves for something new to read I chanced on a thin volume which had been filed backwards, leaving the spine hidden. Stuck fast between two browned, mottled volumes I pulled out a book that I'd never seen before.

The true grimoire: a test of faith

I found the language unfamiliar and jarring and flicking through the pages I decided the book must be very old. Even though it was only a few pages in length, the slim volume was bound in a thick, dark, cracked leather jacket. There was an embossed outline of a horned man on the cover and I felt uneasy holding this unwholesome looking book which felt out of place in the heart of my family home. It didn't feel right. Why had I never seen the book before? With no-one around to tell me otherwise, my curiosity got the better of me and I returned to my bedroom determined to find out more. Sitting cross-legged, I prised the pages open to find a fascinating passage:

Teaching the mode of satisfying one's destiny through the mystery of magik

I quickly became engrossed in this strange text. Skimming through the pages I slowly picked up on the rhythm of the old English and it dawned on me that I'd found a book of spells. I didn't know why, but I felt guilty reading the grimoire. I was sure it had been hidden for a reason. Mulling over the contents, digesting every word as best

I could, my concentration was broken by the sound of footsteps on the landing outside my door. I'd been vaguely aware of someone moving around downstairs, but I was startled all the same when I heard my door handle move. Why do they never knock? I slipped the book under my pillow and pulled the sheets up around my head and pretended to sleep. The door creaked open. I'd been stupid to look at books of magic, it wasn't the Christian thing to do. For a moment no-one entered, but then came a voice, a whisper on the threshold.

'Ann, darling,' It was my mother. 'Did I hear you up and about? Are you feeling OK?'

I pretended that she'd woken me and did my best to look tired and confused, 'Who's that?' I mumbled, 'I must have dozed off.'

When I opened my eyes my mother was sitting beside me on the bed. She was stroking my hair in a way that I remembered as soothing as a child, but which now made me feel a little uneasy. Remembering the book, I worried she might feel the rough edges of the grimoire poking through the pillow. I don't know why I was so afraid, but something told me that the book wasn't meant to be shared.

'I think you're looking much better, Ann.'

I nodded, 'I feel much better now. Maybe I could go outside soon?'

My mother smiled. When she looked at me like this I was sure she thought I could do no wrong. Her guilt about my incident made her want to comfort me. She thought that if she hadn't left me alone then I would never have blacked out at the druids' graves. It would only be a matter of time before she tried to do something for me. I don't know why she did it; maybe to help her feel like more of a mother. In the end it was my old favourite and she brought me milk and buttered bread. Before long I was alone and back with the book.

The grimoire's boasts were many and the passages filled me with fear and wonder. The book contained a number of spells and rites which promised to conjure up your heart's desire, speak to the dead, or win great prizes to make yourself the wealthiest person alive. I lingered on the spells that spoke of 'intercourse' and 'carnal love'. They made me think about Joe and for a while I was caught in a dream.

Later, one page in particular caught my eye. Though only three pages long, there was a lengthy passage on communing with druids which I devoured hungrily, reading it again and again, until I knew it by heart.

Before long I had made up my mind to follow the course of action laid out in this fantastical text. As I looked out of my bedroom window towards the standing stones I saw that my companion was back. The woman in white was waiting.

3

Joe Meek

Ever since they unearthed the metal box at the druids' graves life had been different at the farm. I'd found the Balfours easy company ever since I'd started to work on the farm at 15. That was six years ago and it seemed as if life was changing fast. I was starting to feel uneasy around the family, and with Ann in particular. She was a curious girl at the best of times. Full of life and always looking to get involved, she wouldn't let any task put her off. I'd been impressed when she'd pitched in during last year's storms. Together we'd fought against fierce winds to gather the flock back to the safety of the barn. That seemed a long time ago now and I'd noticed that Ann was spending more time by herself. For the last few days I'd watched from a distance as she slipped away from her daily tasks and disappeared up into the hills. Where are you going, my girl? The thought stayed with me as her father, Davie Balfour, approached, clearly a man with something on his mind.

'She's gone again, Joe. I don't know what to do with her.' He looked tired and his voice was strained, 'Jean's beside herself with worry.'

Davie looked awful. His face was pale and drawn and it looked as if he'd lost weight. It had only been three months since his war hero brother, Charlie, had died in a freak accident in Glasgow and he'd taken it hard, even though he was trying to hide it. Through all the bluster, though, I suspected my benefactor was only looking for a little reassurance. 'She'll be fine, Davie. Probably just a phase she's going through?' I turned to gesture towards the tree line behind, 'I think I saw her going up into the hills a while back.'

'Aye, well she knows about the stones. She isn't happy about it.'

We'd spoken about the job yesterday, although I wasn't convinced the idea was sound. The standing stones were part of a triangle of druidic sites on and around Cuff Hill, with the Rocking Stone not far distant and the druids' graves marking the latest piece of the past to be uncovered. I wondered if all the sites were connected. But it seemed that all the talk of ancient sects had been too much for Davie. He told me he'd been toying with the idea of trying to grow crops, even though all before had failed. Adamant his plan would work he'd asked me to break up the stones to make way for a field. It all seemed orchestrated to destroy the stones, but they were so well known it seemed like madness. I tried to get to the bottom of what was bothering him.

'But why's Ann so interested in the stones? I've never understood the fascination.'

Davie Balfour was running his hands through his hair, the nervous gesture giving away more than he knew, 'I don't know either, Joe, but she's obsessed. Things haven't been right these last few weeks. My brother's death was the start of it all but ever since they uncovered the druids' graves she's been on at me to try and find out more about them. She's always been obsessed with her stories, but this is different. I'm at my wits end with it, Joe. I just don't know how to make her understand that it's all just nonsense.'

I shifted awkwardly, looking down at my feet and tried to change the subject. 'I heard the road's being diverted?'

Davie frowned; he assumed the remark had been made for a reason. He played along, hoping Joe would elaborate, 'Aye, that's right enough. They're saying the site's important – that it warrants further investigation, whatever that means. Now that's high talk for a load of old rubble, if you ask me, but they're taking it seriously. The road's to go a little further south but it won't hold them up for long.'

I listened as Davie havered away, but something didn't make sense. He was holding his cap in hand, wringing it nervously. He was fretting about something and I wanted to know more. Selfishly I thought it might have consequences for me. 'If those graves are too important to disturb, do you think we should be touching the standing stones?'

But as soon as I'd said it I knew I'd gone too far. Davie raised his voice to me for the first time; his face burning red with anger, 'It's my bloody land, Joe, and I'll do whatever the hell I like with it.' He walked off to the perimeter fence trying to suppress a cough, looking north towards the standing stones. I followed suit trying to catch his breathless conversation, 'You don't know what it's been like, Joe. She goes up every day. First to the graves, then the standing stones; I don't know what she does up there, but she's changed. It's like I don't even know my own daughter anymore.'

Davie was never one for getting personal and I felt like I was intruding. Still I felt sure that I was edging closer to the truth. 'Is everything alright?'

Davie smiled back, weakly. He seemed a man resigned to dealing with his daughter alone, 'I appreciate everything you do round here, Joe, but there are a few things happening in the family that I'd like to keep to myself. It's nothing personal. You're a great help around the farm, and I wouldn't be without you. If you could just put your normal routine aside for the day and get to work on the stones I'd be forever in your debt.'

Davie's body language had changed and his shoulders slumped forward as he traipsed off round the back of the farmhouse. He said he'd get me the sledgehammer. I waited by the front door when Jean came out to meet me.

'Are you alright there, Joe? It looks like you've seen a ghost.' She was smiling, something that made me happy, although I knew I'd never tell her to her face.

'Not too bad. I couldn't say the same for your man, though. Is he doing OK?'

I saw Jean tense slightly, 'What do you mean, Joe? He's as well as he's ever been.'

I nodded, muttering something I only half caught myself. Jean always made me feel a little confused. 'He seems worried about Ann?'

Jean's eyes narrowed. She wasn't used to me being so forward, and I wasn't sure she approved. I was still young, only 21, and the only reason I was there was to do the work. All the same I couldn't help but moon around after her, always trying to catch her attention by taking on extra jobs. And me less than half her age; who was I trying to kid? Jean seemed to sense my unease, 'I'll worry enough for the both of us, Joe. Don't you be fretting on my account.'

I was going to apologise. I felt as though I'd gone too far. Jean's demeanour had changed and I cursed myself for even thinking about overstepping the mark. But the moment was gone and in the background I heard the hacking cough which announced Davie's return. 'My God, Davie, that cough's not getting any better. Have you been to see the doctor?'

'I'll be fine, Joe. You know what I'm like with these things. But it'll pass. It always does.'

I had a lot of time for Davie. It had been him that had first given me work. I'd been a boy back then and the family had needed help. Threepwood now felt as much a part of my life as it was for the Balfours. Still, even though I was proud to know them, the sad truth was that we'd never really been that close. Ann had been different, though, she was more like a sister and it pained me to see her in trouble. I cared about the family and I knew that Davie wasn't being honest about his health. His coughing had been getting gradually worse for several weeks, ever since he'd started talking about trying his hand at growing crops. I'd caught him using a handkerchief to cover his mouth more than once.

I'd seen TB before; such an ugly disease. I could just about remember my younger brother but he hadn't lasted long – spitting out his last in a damp infested slum. I hoped I was wrong, that the vile leveller hadn't found its way into my life again, but it would explain why Ann had been behaving so strangely. I jumped as Davie handed me the sledgehammer, and noticed that Jean was staring at me.

'And you can leave my Jean well alone, young man. There's work enough to be done without your flirting.' He stood smiling, with the hammer in hand. I nodded red-faced and sloped off to work.

The standing stones weren't far away, maybe two miles from the farmhouse, midway between the graves and the Rocking Stone. I hoped I wouldn't meet any walkers. Those busybodies from town had too much time on their hands, rambling for fun, when they should be out working like the rest of us. It was the questions that annoyed me the most, with their easy manner and nosey inclinations. But I was worried. I knew that if I ran into any of them today I'd struggle to explain why I was smashing the standing stones to smithereens. I do as I'm told, though, because it's not my land. More to the point, if I don't work, I'll starve.

When I set off it was hard going and the elements were against me. It had rained heavily last night, and the wet ground was making the climb up the hill trickier than usual. The weight of the sledgehammer unbalanced me and I slipped and fell several times on the way up, cursing my clumsiness. At the summit, finally, I stopped to rest. In the distance I could see the farmhouse, nestled at the brow of a hill which looked across Kirkleegreen Reservoir, easy to spot with a tiny island on its western edge. I watched from the summit and saw Davie taking the cattle out to pasture, herding them with his collie and crook; all part of the daily routine. I snacked on porridge chipped from the hardened block from the kitchen drawer, trying to avoid getting to the task at hand, when I saw someone else about a mile off. Although I couldn't make out the figure clearly, I was sure it was Ann; her distinctive blue dress with white collar marked her out against the mossy hillside. I thought she had a dog with her at first but as she came closer I saw that she was leading a goat behind her. It looked like Rickerton, Davie's pride and joy. Where's she going with that? Ann had left the site of the druids' graves, which was strewn with broken rocks from the recent road works. Judging by her path she was heading towards the stones, so I continued my watch, curious about what she might do next. Davie and Jean certainly wanted to know what was troubling their daughter and this seemed a good opportunity to learn more. I stepped back and scanned the horizon as Ann darted across the field and turned up towards the stones. I followed at a distance.

About quarter of an hour later I saw something that I couldn't explain.

The standing stones had stood for more than 5,000 years but if you asked a local, the historical details were sketchy at best, with several conflicting versions of 'the truth.' One legend had it that they had been put in place by sun worshippers, before being adopted by the druids some two millennia later. Many myths had sprung up through the years about what might have happened there. Some said human sacrifices had been made to appease the old Gods, while others had it that the stones were used for spiritual reasons. I knew the truth of it though. I knew that no-one had the faintest idea about what had really happened. I wondered what Ann expected to find there, what truth she sought.

I watched from a safe distance behind a thicket of spindly birch trees, where I had a good view of the stone circle. I noticed the animal first. The goat had been draped in flowers, with a green and pink garland slung across its neck. I could see the animal, Rickerton, was tied by a short rope to a stake in the centre of the stone circle. He seemed distressed, bleating repeatedly as if expecting danger. Ann was building a fire with wood gathered from the surrounding thickets. She worked quickly and lit the branches with matches as flames teased the kindling to life. I wondered how the wood had managed to stay so dry; it had been raining so heavily. But as the smoke turned black I reasoned the twigs must have been gathered in a hurry. For a moment, I lost sight of Ann as she moved to the far side of the fire, her body masked by the billowing blanket of smoke. When she came back into view I saw that she had pulled her dress down past one arm, with her sleeves hanging awkwardly. I almost cried out for her to cover herself but I couldn't help but watch; her dancing held me in a spell. My reverie was abruptly shattered when she stunned me into silence. The sunlight glanced off something metallic. Ann had a knife. She was shouting something and I tried to follow her words over the crackle of the fire and the grunts of the agitated beast.

'I offer you this victim, oh Gods, both old and new. May this honour, glory and powerful spirit placate your needs and deliver unto me, that which I seek. May the blood of this victim make this so, and for you to accept these ashes.'

I watched silently as Ann straddled the goat and grabbed it, before sliding the blade round the animal's neck and slicing its throat, the blood spurting into the open fire. That was only the beginning and she started to hack away at the poor beast, skinning the animal before throwing its remains on the fire, which was now well alight. Ann was laughing and dancing round the fire, holding the bloodied pelt. I didn't know what to do and sat there transfixed as the little girl I'd known was transformed into a monster.

About an hour later Ann left with the goatskin, apparently happy to let the fire peter out. I couldn't see how she could return home covered in blood. What's she thinking, doing these horrific things so close to home? Her father was right; the girl had changed, but why? I picked up my pace to try and catch her up but she'd started to run. I followed suit, shouting out her name on the move, but she didn't hear me, or if she did she didn't turn round. The reservoir wasn't too far away and I realised that she might be heading for the rocky outcrop which towered over the water. Out of breath I reached the bluff which looked out across the water just in time to see her jump off the side and drop down with a splash some 20 feet below. Frantic with worry, I was going to jump in after her when I saw that she'd discarded her clothes. I could hear her sing while she swam. I knew I couldn't speak to her now, it wouldn't be proper, but again I had thoughts about the girl that I hadn't expected, a knot gnawing away at my stomach. I didn't know what to do – is this something that Davie should know about? Looking back towards the standing stones I saw the thin wisps of grey smoke form a grimy canopy above the birch grove on top of Cuff Hill.

In the end I decided that I'd do Ann a favour and went back to honour her father's wishes. I'd make light work of destroying what evidence remained of the abhorrent ritual I'd seen that day, something I was struggling to forget. Half an hour later, with sledgehammer in hand, I started to pound relentlessly at the ancient standing stones. By the end of the day I wanted to be sure that no-one would ever know they'd existed. Tired and weary I walked back to the farm, determined to see things right.

4

Jean Balfour

I felt that I'd humoured Davie for long enough; his coughing was louder and more frequent. Whatever was wrong with him wasn't clearing up on its own.

'You need to get yourself to the hospital, love. I'm worried about you.'

Davie bristled. In an effort to avoid the question he busied himself moving coal from the porch floor to the scuttle, 'Away with you, woman. There's nothing wrong with me that fresh air and some peace and quiet won't solve.'

I was angry. I'd tried to talk to him countless times and he'd fobbed me off, again and again. 'Will you listen to me for once, man? You're not well and you know it. Ann knows it too.' I stopped to catch my breath. I'd been louder with him than I'd meant to be. Trying to sound calm, I lowered my voice but continued to press, 'I think that's why she's been acting so strangely. I'd have scolded her before now, but I'm scared for you myself.'

Davie continued to avoid the issue. He paused; the clatter of coal dropping to the floor brought an unnatural silence to the room. Moving close, he whispered that everything would be fine, but my patience was gone. 'YOU'RE NOT FINE AND YOU KNOW IT.'

'There's no need to raise your voice with me.'

I reached out to Davie and grabbed his shoulders roughly, 'Davie, love. You need to go to hospital and get this seen to.'

'How many times must I repeat myself, there's NOTHING WRONG WITH ME!'

The stress of his outburst set off his coughing again and Davie doubled over in agony, struggling for breath. I could only offer my love. I put my arms around him and tried to reassure him, but my words did nothing to help. Davie looked down at the hands that had been covering his mouth and revealed the blood that I'd feared he'd been hiding for some time.

'It's too late for the Doctor, Jean. I've already been.' There were no tears or remorse, just a simple resignation, 'We don't have the money for treatment, and certainly not at this late stage.'

The words hit hard. I knew that Davie lived his life for our family and it was all falling apart, and for what? 'There must be something...'

'There isn't, pet.' Davie was shaking his head. 'I wish there was, but there just isn't.'

***

Ann had been sitting listening at the top of the stairs and had heard every word. It confirmed what she already knew and made her certain she was doing the right thing. Ann knew her father was ill and she'd been working on a way to make it better. She wouldn't accept that they were out of options. Ann had hoped that a million clever ways to beat the illness would flash through her mind, but in the end there was only one thing she could think of that might do any good. Ann made up her mind to return to her ritual and to see it through to the end. She just hoped her father would still be around for the festival of Samhain.

Joe Meek

I knew a thing or two about the standing stones and the old ways. The experts said the basaltic greenstone had been quarried from a site a few miles south and dragged into position. Cursing the druids' choice of material I had to admit that they certainly knew what they'd been doing. The stones didn't go quietly, with jagged chips scratching my face as I swung wildly with the sledgehammer. Eventually, though, the constant, furious force made its mark and the rocks were slowly ground down, their mysteries obliterated for all time.

Davie had asked me to use the shrapnel to repair the dry stone wall around the Rocking Stone, and I'd been shifting the rubble for days. Parts of the wall had been knocked over by grazing cattle and people out walking. The strips of the standing stones were a perfect match to patch the perimeter round the Rocking Stone. Getting them from A to B however was another matter, with an uneven mile separating the two sites. It was open field all the way, but the marshy hilltop didn't make for easy passage. Each trip took me several hours, with the weight of the load being borne by back. It gave me time to think, though. I hadn't mentioned anything about what I'd seen with Ann that day, of the horror of her sacrifice, but I felt certain that removing the stones was the right thing to do. I was almost finished when I saw a figure at the site of the standing stones, running frantically and screaming. I knew long before she reached me that it was Ann. I could see that she wasn't happy.

'What have you done, Joe?' Ann was spinning round trying to gather up chunks of rock, as if she could piece the stones back together, 'This is vandalism. How could you destroy such an ancient site? Do you know what you've done?'

She was hysterical; her voice was wavering; her agitation plain to see. I knew she cared about the spot. Even before the 'incident' she had always asked questions about the history of the place. But that was all in the past, and it was about time she knew it.

'Your father wants the land cleared for crops, and that's what I've done.' I paused for a second wondering if I should bring it all up, but in my heart I knew I had no choice, 'I saw what you did here, Ann Balfour. I know it all, but don't you worry, because I haven't told a soul.' I was finding it hard to catch my breath, the tension of the moment was making me nervous, 'You should think yourself lucky for that, because if your father knew, he'd be as angry as hell.'

Ann calmed down and gave me a knowing look. 'I saw you there that day, Joe.' She said. 'I knew you were watching me. Did you like to see me that way? Maybe your blood was up; you haven't thought of me like that before have you?'

It was like she was reading my mind, but I had been certain I'd been well hidden. I couldn't let her turn the tables.

'You don't know what you're saying, Ann. I know you were alone, save for that poor animal. I told your father it had escaped and fell in the water and drowned – all those lies just to protect you.' I was struggling to meet her gaze, the fury in her eyes more unsettling than I could ever have expected from one so young. I didn't want to confront her, but she had to know I was there to protect her. 'I don't want any trouble at the house, especially not from you. I feel bad now, telling you all those stories about the druids. All stuff and nonsense and you've gone too far. It's not right what you did.'

'I think you liked what I did. I know what you were thinking about me.' Ann was smiling in a way that made me blush. She didn't seem to notice and continued to talk. 'But you've made a mistake, Joe. It's not the time for that. You know that my father's not well; he might die. What you don't understand is that the stones might just have been his best chance of recovery. I suppose you've got that on your conscience now.' She smiled at me again, this time it was more of a manic grin, 'It's lucky for you that there are other options.'

I watched as Ann circled round me, watching me intently. She'd picked up a piece of long grass and was wrapping it around her index finger; I could see the flesh turn white and red where the reed dug deep. She kept talking and the more she said the more worried I became.

'There are things about this land, Joe, that you don't know anything about. But I know. The lady of the woods shows me things.'

I couldn't help but laugh aloud, 'The Lady of Threepwood? That's just a story.'

'Is it?' Ann was looking past me, her gaze focused somewhere in the distance. Her next words changed everything, 'Then who's that behind you?'

When I turned around I was dazzled by a flash. A sharp pain passed through me like a wave of fear, as a figure in white flew at me from a copse of birch trees. Both arms were outstretched and I saw anger in her eyes. But it was the scream that closed me down. The noise was unlike anything I'd heard before, like ten people crying out in agony. As the figure flew at me at astonishing speed my legs gave way and I fell, hitting my head off the remnants of the standing stones. It was all over as quickly as it had begun and I was knocked out cold.

When I came to, it was dark. My head was sore and feeling a damp patch under my hair I found that I was bleeding. That night was like no other and as I slowly made my way back, I froze to the spot as the farmhouse came into sight. There it was again, as plain as day. Impossibly, there was a glowing figure in white approaching the farm over the water. I couldn't explain what was happening but I knew Ann was in trouble. I hoped I wouldn't be too late; this wasn't how it was meant to end.

5

Ann Balfour

Under the night sky I saw the luminous figure standing way out on the reservoir, hovering above the water. It was an impossible sight, which filled me with a curious horror.

What does she want from me? I watched as the spectre edged closer. With every blink of my eyes the Lady of Threepwood flashed closer to the farmhouse. So far, every time I'd seen her she'd kept her distance but for some reason, tonight was different. I felt no great animosity from the Lady and was strangely relaxed when she appeared, something that had been happening more and more these last few days. I glanced back at the bed and saw the grimoire waiting. I had all but memorised the book's spell and I knew what to do. The goat skin was still bloodied and wet from the sacrifice, but I'd drawn the runic symbols as outlined in the text as best as I could. All that I needed now was to go to the Rocking Stone and see this wretched affair through. After that it would be plain sailing and my Dad would get well. I have to do it for him no matter what the risks are.

I'd stored the pelt under the mattress and lifted the thin cover to retrieve it. It was rough with mottled blood, but I persevered and rolled it up and prepared to leave.

Looking out, I saw the moon was masked by heavy cloud, and inside my bedroom was pitch black. We had no electricity and I chided myself for having snuffed out the candle too early. Scrabbling about by my bedside table I found the matches but, agitated, knocked my candle over, then heard it roll off out of sight under my bed. I was scared and sweating with tension, and cursed my stupid mistake. Eventually, I managed to replace the candle but I knew my clumsiness was losing me time. I moved to the window where the light was better. I struck the match and tipped the wick over to meet the flame, being careful not to burn myself, and watched as the candle flared into life. I was mesmerised for a second as the dull glow spread through the room.

CRACK.

I jumped. What was that? It sounded like a pebble being cast at the window. More followed shortly after, in three short blasts. CRACK. CRACK. CRACK.

The darkness amplified the sound in the dead of night and my earlier calm gave way to a very real fear. It was close to midnight and the house was still. I knew my parents wouldn't be outside throwing stones at my window. Could it be Joe? If it was he might not be safe. There was no-one else here. I jumped again, as the single barrage gave way to a crescendo above. The sound grew louder, almost deafening, like gravel being poured on the corrugated iron roof. The sprattle and scrape of stone on metal made a horrific noise which made me feel dizzy and sick. Perhaps I'm being stupid? It might just as easily be hail. I started to laugh at my nerves. Mother would be so cross if she could see me like this. Turning, finally, I looked back out the window. The air went from my lungs and I forgot to breathe. The Lady of Threepwood was standing right in front of me, closer than ever before. The legend sometimes had her as an old hag, but she was no old lady, rather a young woman with a familiar smile. Her dark brown eyes looked tired but there was a warmth to her face that I hadn't expected, having seen her from a distance so many times before.

'What do you want of me my lady? Have you come to help?' She smiled at me again and I felt reassured once more, sensing again that she meant me no harm. They said that her appearance brought bad luck and death, but I had seen her many times already and nothing bad had happened. I'd come to no obvious harm. I thought then that perhaps she meant to help. 'Can you help me to save my family? For my father's sake, you must.'

The lady said nothing but turned and faded back to the silence outside. She seemed to pass through the walls and when I rushed to the window I could see her waiting down in the courtyard. Silently I took the grimoire and the goat skin and tip-toed down the creaking stairs, before slipping open the latch to the side door. I looked back before leaving. Our collie, Stan, lifted his head for a second but, when he saw it was me, did nothing more. He was whimpering, though, and I wondered if he sensed more than I gave him credit for, 'Don't worry, boy, she's not here for you, it's me she wants.'

I opened the door as the cloud cover lifted and in the distance the sharp moonlight illuminated the tall birch circle that formed a perimeter around the Rocking Stone on the top of Cuff Hill. I no longer trusted my eyes and it seemed as if the circle was aflame, with the canopy burning bright into the night. It was then that I remembered the rhyme:

If you come to see her once, take heed,
she won't be far from home.
She shall not stop, she'll seek you out,
from the fire of the Rocking Stone.

Whether I was going mad I didn't know, but I knew I'd been chosen for something. I felt sure it made sense to continue. After the spell had been cast, I'd know for certain. It was only a matter of time.

6

Joe Meek

I ran as fast as I could. By the time I reached the farmhouse I knew something was wrong. Inside, paraffin lamps lit up the kitchen. I heard a commotion inside, as if the place was being ransacked. Trying to think what to do, I scanned the courtyard, worried that I might have unwelcome company. It can't be a burglary; too rare in these parts, but you never know. The noise stopped, just for a second, and a violent bang rang out as if someone, or something, had fallen. I could place it now, the noise was coming from the hallway and I knew I had to go in. Sidling up to the front porch, I was scared about what I might find. But by the time I reached the threshold, it was a familiar face that met me.

'Jean, thank God it's you. I was worried something had happened.'

She was in no mood to listen, 'There's something wrong with Davie. He can't catch his breath and he's taken a fall. I need help.'

I'd never seen her so rattled; her eyes were darting from side to side, with a crazed look for company. I tried to keep up but she was talking at a hundred miles an hour, 'I tried to wake Ann, but she's not here. Have you seen her?' Jean was looking back inside the house and then back past me and out into the courtyard. Maybe she was trying to decide what to do; take care of her husband or look for her daughter? It was a near impossible choice. I reached out and took her arm.

'Take the truck and get Davie to hospital. It's slow but it'll get you there. Don't worry about Ann, she won't be far away. I'll go and find her and keep her here until you get back.' I squeezed her hand in a way I hoped she found reassuring, but even in the dark of the courtyard I could see that Jean was terrified. I tried to think what else I could do to help and believe me, if I had the money to spare, I'd have paid for a doctor myself. But it was times like these that were the great reality check. We were all just farmers, scraping a living off the land and people like us don't have the luxury of expensive medical help. Jean knew she had no other choice.

'Just bring her back, Joe. Ann will want to be with her father when she finds out. I'll need to travel to Paisley for help, but it'll take time, especially on these roads at night.'

Jean was starting to hyperventilate and I saw that she was clutching her chest, as her breathing quickened. She needed to try and calm down if she was going to drive, 'Do you need a hand getting into the car? You said he'd fallen.' Not waiting for an answer, I walked past her and looked through the door. Davie was sitting on the second bottom step. He had blood on his mouth and I couldn't be sure if it was from the coughing or the fall.

'You're going to be alright, Davie. Jean's going to take you to the doctor, and you're not to worry about Ann. She's not far away. I saw her not 20 minutes ago. I'll bring her back, you'll see.'

I squeezed his hand for comfort but the fight had left Davie and he mumbled thanks to me as I helped Jean drag him to the car like a sack of coal. I waited to see them off. Jean held back to say said she'd send a telegram to the farm for 12 tomorrow, and asked me to be here to receive it.

I watched as they drove off and then went looking for Ann. In the distance I could see the occasional glimmer of light cutting through the woods on Cuff Hill. I didn't know what she was doing, but I thanked my lucky stars that she was still close by.

Ann Balfour

The hill was normally easy enough to climb but it was hard going in the dead of night, and the Rocking Stone was still a way off. Holding the large metal paraffin lamp to light the way was unbalancing me in the dark of the night, with the sheep's droppings and cow dung turning the hill into an unwelcome helter skelter. I grasped at the long grass and low hanging branches to try and stay upright, but I still fell several times. I could feel the small cuts from thorns and branches start to sting my hands, arms and legs, but I had to carry on. Looking back I could see the family had finally woken up and the lights were on back at the farm. I must have been noisier than I thought; maybe the dog gave me away after all. It won't be long now. I tried to keep the lamplight low so that I wouldn't be seen from the house, but as I stumbled on along the uneven embankment the old lamp swung wildly and I couldn't be sure if I'd given myself away.

Finally, I broke through the tree line and stopped for a moment on the exposed fields on the top of Cuff Hill. I could see the birch circle around the Rocking Stone silhouetted in the moonlight. It wasn't far now, only about half a mile. The worst of the journey was over. Checking the goat skin for damage, I smiled. It was still safely tucked away in the hessian grain sack, along with the rest of the paraphernalia the book dictated I'd need. Sloshing through the streams and mud I trudged across the barren hill top before resting at the perimeter wall. The day had turned to Samhain and I knew what I had to do.

In the distance the Lady of Threepwood was waiting.

Joe Meek

I'd lost sight of the lantern and thought Ann might have gone to the druids' graves; a spot she'd been fascinated with ever since they'd been uncovered all those weeks ago. By the time I'd filled another lantern and left the farm I knew that Ann would be well ahead.

I jogged along as fast as I dared in the dark, sticking to the path wherever I could, and cursing as the boggiest sections held me up. The coarse material of my waterlogged trousers started to chafe as I walked, and I winced as my skin became raw with the constant rubbing. I cursed my intuition when I made it to the graves, the first stop on the way up the hill, as there was no sign of life. So I made my way north, over the brow of the hill towards the Rocking Stone. I hoped that she had no more mad schemes up her sleeve, and shuddered when I thought about what she'd done to that poor old goat. Please, let there be no more of that.

***

Overhead the cirrus clouds shifted quickly under north-westerly winds, with the moonlight casting strange shadows across the ancient woodland. In the background, birds shifted uneasily in the undulating branches. At the reservoir, the water in the weir streamed steadily down as if trying to quiet the night with a constant shush. In response the clouds dissolved and the night was clear, with constellations coming into sharp focus as clear sight was granted.

Such was the night of the Rocking Stone.

Ann Balfour

Tired, wet, and breathless I was relieved when I finally reached my destination. I spread the goatskin over the top of the Rocking Stone and climbed up onto the shaking platform, placing myself at its centre. Careful not to tip the balance I breathed in and out until I started to feel light headed, just as the grimoire dictated. All around me the trees, doused in paraffin from the lamp, burned brightly, with the atmosphere transformed as the ritual began.

'Oh great Gods who created man to live fully in this world and the other, look kindly on me and permit union with the rebel spirits. Let me possess the treasures that were formed by your hands for earthly needs. Give me the faculty to possess your wisdom and show me the way through the words of the ancients.'

The flames in the trees burned higher, and despite the dampness of the night and the soaking trees, the wood hissed its compliance as the temperature continued to rise.

'I implore you mistress of the woods and masters of the rebel spirits to hear me now. I implore you to abandon your dwelling, in whatever part of the world you should be, to come to me now. I command you by the sacrifice I have made, and as the great Gods command, by the power of the precious blood that has been spilled. Speak now spirit. Speak now.'

I waited and watched. The fire had spread from the trees to the long grass and all around me it raged hot and fast, forming a ring around the Rocking Stone. I kept repeating the chants, again and again, for the great Gods and the Lady of Threepwood. Gradually, the figures formed. First as nothing more than flickers in the flames, and then slowly they appeared – a ring of hooded figures around the stone; life from the lifeless. My cries had been heard, and I knew the stone had answered my plea. It was the woman in white who came to me first, as I knew it would be. This indomitable figure had stalked the hills, bringing death to the uninitiated. I was certain she was here to help. But something wasn't right. Her smile was gone and her face was contorted and pained, lines slashing through the flesh as fire flicked out from under her skin. She loped through the scorching heat and her body lit up like a firework; sparks starting a chain reaction through the circle as the landscape disintegrated before me. It was then that she spoke, for the first and only time. Her judgment was clear.

'There are 50 years allowed before the reckoning, and this is not your time. You sought new life and it will come. But the price is paid, your judgement set.'

My life would never be the same again.

7

Peggy Balfour, 1953

'But where was Joe during all this?' I asked. It was a good story and my mother, Ann, had put her heart and soul into her performance. She was very convincing, so much so that she'd scared me half to death. I jumped when she snapped back to the here and now.

'Well Peggy, there's the thing. Joe found me lying behind the Rocking Stone and took me home. He's always been adamant there was no sign of fire, and that wet wood can't burn. He said it must have all been in my head.'

'But you knew different?'

My mother paused for a second before continuing, 'I thought I did. I was convinced that the spectre had told me that I'd be allowed 50 years more, whatever that meant, but nothing ever happened. After that I never saw the Lady of Threepwood again, and I never went back to the Rocking Stone.'

'Because of what happened to Grandpa?'

Mother was stroking my hair; her eyes misted over as she thought back to the real drama that night, 'It was the night he died. My poor old Mum didn't make it far. She told me later that she'd tried to console your Grandpa in the truck, but he was dead by the time they reached the hospital. She sat with him for hours at the top of the braes. There was nothing to be done for him.' Her eyes had lost their focus, it seemed she'd said too much and quickly tried to change the subject, 'But things were different after that and I forgot about druids and the Rocking Stone. My mother never spoke of it either, God bless her. It had all been for nothing, just a silly childish fancy and not worth the telling. You should never have asked me.'

I could see my mother was upset and I felt guilty for bringing it all up; but the story held a grim fascination for me. I was always sure there was something she didn't want to tell me. 'It's a very sad story, mother.' I stopped to lift the poker and was stabbing at the fading coals, trying to eke out our evening just a little bit longer, 'What do you think she meant by allowing you 50 years before the reckoning?'

'She meant nothing at all, because it was all just a story. The doctors told me that it was all in my head. That what the story really meant was that I wanted my father to live a long healthy life and that I must have subconsciously known that he wasn't well. It's only natural, don't you think? I was just a girl, like you. What did I know?'

My efforts to rekindle the fire came to nothing after that and the flames ebbed to embers. My mother made me a glass of hot milk and sent me to bed. As I lay there that night I thought it was strange that we still lived in the same farmhouse, and it was eerie to think my mother had conjured up her fantastic experience in this very room. The thought sustained me and I was unable to rest. Exhausted through my sleepless night I knocked on the next door along the hall and climbed into bed with my mother. She smiled and said I was too old for it now, but I knew she felt lonely too. She always seemed somehow distant, and I felt she watched me a little too closely at times. She was probably just being over protective.

That night we slept as a storm drew near, not knowing then what lay ahead. Outside the wind rose and the metal roof strained to remain fixed in the rafters. In the end it wouldn't really matter. The future had already been written.

Part 2

8

Peggy, 1983

You knew her as Ann, but to me she just was just plain old Mum. You've heard about her younger years but I'm afraid that's all in the past. Mum died on the 23rd of October 1983. She was only 63. I was at home with the family when I got the news. It should have been a mundane call, interrupting a night by the telly. But it was more than that; it was a call that changed my life.

We'd been laughing at our favourite programme, a hidden camera show, when the phone started to rattle on the table in the hall. No-one wanted to move. I remember I couldn't take my eyes off the TV. The host was dressed as a policeman and berating one of the show's victims about illegally parking his open-top car. Behind them a van load of manure was being piled through the roof. It was slapstick and silly, but we never missed an episode. Try as we did to ignore the phone, it kept on ringing. Eventually I gave in and crossed out into the hall, fully intending to tell them to bugger off. It turned out that I didn't have time. My caller got straight to the point.

'Can I speak to Peggy, please?'

It was a disembodied, tinny voice. I tried to work out who it was, but I was distracted still and glancing back at the show. As the stranger continued to cut through the informality he quickly gained my full attention, the words dissolving into a jumbled mass, jarring at my consciousness as he tried to reach me, to make me understand. In truth, I can't remember much of the detail. I'd just seen Mum two weeks ago and she'd been fine. We were planning our Christmas; but now... I was twisting the curved coil of plastic telephone cable round my fingers, pulling at it absentmindedly. When the call ended I went back and watched the rest of the programme, although I couldn't really concentrate. Later when Maggie and Martin had gone to bed, John asked who'd rung, said I'd been awfully quiet. It was only then, that the news hit home.

'It was the family doctor, Mr Ranscombe.'

'Ranscombe?' John looked at me confused, 'He's not our doctor.'

John could be slow at times but it wasn't fair to lay any of this on him. I persevered, trying to figure out what to say, daring myself to even think it out loud. 'Gavin Ranscombe – my Mum's doctor.'

He said 'oh' and picked up the TV Times to see what was coming up next, 'What did he want then? Has the old witch taken a turn or something?'

I stopped for a second. It felt like I was standing at the edge of a cliff, willing myself to jump. Once I went over there'd be no turning back. Then it happened. Three words to change the world.

'She's dead, John.'

He stopped flipping through the magazine and looked round, not knowing what to say. I kept talking so he didn't have to, 'The Doctor said she died this afternoon. He said he'd have phoned earlier but he couldn't from her house.' Always bloody refusing to get a phone. Infuriating woman. 'I've lost count of the number of times I told her she needed to get connected, but she wouldn't listen.'

John's cogs were starting to turn, slowly but perceptibly. 'Dead, but how?' he said, ever the blunt instrument, 'We just saw her the other week,' He knew he'd been offhand and was trying to make up for it.

'He said it looked like a heart attack. He said old Joe found her sitting in the living room, staring out into the hills.'

'Old Joe?'

'For God's sake, John – just listen!' At times like these, his mental capacity seemed to narrow, limited to repeating key phrases, like a malfunctioning robot on borrowed time. In fairness, though, he seemed more shocked by the news than I was. I tried to break it to him as gently as I could, 'Joe still kept an eye out for Mum. He doted on her; they became so close, you know that. The doctor said Joe had taken a trip up to visit the farm. It was him that found her.'

'Is she still there?'

'No, John,' I said patiently, 'She's been taken to the hospital for a post-mortem. What they expect to find, I just don't know. She was always so healthy.'

John was starting to understand, a glimmer of sense shone through as he finally engaged his brain and started to speak in coherent sentences, the first perfectly pitched to strike me while I was down, 'Well I must say you're taking this very well. It's your own mother we're talking about here. What do we need to do?'

I didn't know why, but he was making me angrier with every word. I wanted to be alone but here I was trapped with my family, 'You don't need to do anything. I'll take care of this. I'm going to go to the house tonight, though, and I'd like to go by myself.'

John stood up, clearly worried, 'Are you sure that's a good idea?'

'I need some time to be alone, and I'll feel close to her there.' I watched him as he frowned, unconvinced. I'd seen this look before. His arms folded in a defensive position and I sat back and waited for the next salvo. I didn't have long to wait.

'I don't know how I feel about you being away up there on your own, especially after what's just happened. Won't you be freaked out? You know what you're like?'

Cheeky sod, but I'm not going to rise to it. Stay calm. 'Thanks, John, but I'll be fine. I'll come back tomorrow, and we can work out what needs to be done.'

I kissed him on the forehead and told him things would be fine and not to worry about Maggie and Martin too much until we knew exactly what to say. But in truth, I wasn't sure what to do. There was something nagging at me that I couldn't remember, something that seemed important. Perhaps something Mum had said? Had she been ill and concealed it, like my Grandpa? No, I'd have noticed that, and she was fighting fit. It would take about 45 minutes to drive down to the farmhouse. I threw some things in a bag and got ready to leave.

Later, on the road, I flicked on the radio looking for distraction and dialled through the crackling channels. There was nothing to hold my attention: a news report on power cuts; classical music; and a conversation about nuclear weapons. On the commercial channel David Bowie said he wanted to dance, but I wasn't in the mood. I switched it off and travelled in silence, the cats' eyes sending tracers into the night, lighting the way back home. I knew Joe was still at the farm and I needed to talk. I had so many questions.

When Joe opened the door it seemed as if he hadn't changed. He worked on the farm into his late sixties and although older now, he was still very much part of the family. I could see that he'd been crying when he opened the door. Somehow that set me off.

'Oh, Joe,' I said tears streaming down my cheeks, the sweet agony of release making it hard to breathe as my body forgot how to function. He held me there in the threshold of my old home. His embrace was comforting, and I knew he felt my mother's loss just as keenly as I did.

'Come inside, lass.' His voice was thick with emotion. I followed him inside.

For a few moments he left me alone in the living room but when he came back he had company; two large whiskies. I smiled and took the tumbler, bracing myself for the warm shock of alcohol that would follow. As I slugged it back the spirits burned my throat, so much so that I gagged and almost spat it back out. 'Jesus, Joe, where the hell did you get this?'

'Home brew,' He was swirling his shot, trying not to smile, 'bit strong is it, Peggy?'

I laughed out loud. He'd been trying to strike the right balance for years with his casks and measures, but staring down at the heavy crystal glass I still wasn't sure he'd cracked it. 'Bit 'tart' perhaps,' I said, placing the glass on the table, 'I think I might just stick to tea.'

We sat in silence for a while, neither wanting to be the first to start talking, but I knew I couldn't stay sitting around for long.

'Did she look peaceful, Joe?'

He bent over and took my hand, 'She looked like she'd slipped off to sleep. She'd been reading an old book by the hearth. When I found her it was sitting on her lap, like she'd rested for a moment between chapters. If I'm honest, she seemed completely at ease. There was absolutely no sign of pain, so don't you worry about that. It's just that—'

'—But it was so sudden!' I blurted it out. I couldn't understand why this had happened, 'Were there no signs that something was wrong?'

Joe looked confused, 'I don't follow you.'

'Come on, Joe. You knew all that stuff she was always going on about up in the hills? The old tales of Threepwood never seemed to leave her.'

Joe nodded. He looked uncomfortable that I'd brought the topic up. Perhaps he thought he'd heard the last of it. 'It's true that we talked about it a lot when we were younger, but...'

He stopped and turned his back to me, and looked as if he was thinking about leaving the room.

'There's something you're not telling me, Joe.'

His next words felt considered which really wasn't like him. 'She'd been going back up there again recently, Peggy. Quite a few times, actually. It's true that she hadn't set foot up there for years, since before you were born in fact, but something was drawing her back. I couldn't ask her about it, though. She'd pretend I wasn't there. When she was like that, well, it was like I barely knew her.'

I knew Mum had been obsessed by the old stories. She was convinced that she was physically part of the landscape; that something malignant was waiting for her. She often spoke of destiny but it always seemed like another of her old fireside stories – colourful, but nothing much more than a flight of fancy. I tried to remember. Fragments of the old story were starting to come back, but none of that could be relevant now, could it? Stirred from my reveries I looked up find to a Joe I'd never seen before – he was terrified.

9

I looked at Joe for what felt like a long time, waiting patiently for him to elaborate, but it seemed he had nothing more to add. 'You're telling me that my mother was going back up to the Rocking Stone, alone?'

'No-one was more surprised than me, Peggy.' Joe looked sheepish, like he'd let loose a secret. 'I know she said she'd never go back, but your Mother had started to obsess over the old stories. It was like she was a girl again.'

I looked out of the window and up to the circle of trees that marked out the perimeter of the Rocking Stone. The canopy swayed under the moonlight and I could not deny its pull. The stone had fascinated my family for decades but there was nothing more to it than fireside folktales. Even so, I was struggling to accept that my mother would have gone back there given the very real fear she'd developed about the place after the death of my Grandpa, 'She lived here her whole life and I cannot once remember her going over the wall and up to the stone.'

'You're right. She refused to go back after she held her ritual; convinced she'd caused the death of her own father, the victim of a curse that she didn't understand. We found her up there, blacked out. Rumours started and people seemed happy to think she was simple. So she tried to make things better, but she didn't do it right. She turned to mysticism and the occult. She said she had always seen the Lady of Threepwood; that she'd kept an eye on her all these years.'

I snorted, despite myself, 'Come on, Joe. You don't believe any of that old crap, do you?'

Joe wouldn't look me in the eye. He was staring hard at the floorboards, trying to conjure up his dignity from somewhere between the cracks, but all he found was a whisper. 'I only know what I saw.'

'Oh please, not this again, Joe. It was fun when I was young, but she's dead now and I need to know the truth. Do you really expect me to believe that you went up there all those years ago and rescued my mother? If you listened to her she was swept away by a ring of fire, after trying to conjure up a tribe of long lost druids! Do you have any idea how crazy that sounds?' I turned away trying to make sense of the conversation, 'I thought I knew you better than that. My mother was young and she was trying to cope with my Grandpa's illness. It dogged her for years, but she got over it.'

Joe had composed himself into a sitting sneer. He looked disgusted and spat out his words, the vitriol aimed squarely in my direction, 'She'd never have discussed it with you.' He was pointing right at me, his old fingers quivering in a decrepit rage. 'She knew what you thought.' Joe gestured behind me at the couch, 'To you, it was just an exciting story for bedtime.' I followed his lead. He was pointing at the same old chairs. Threadbare through decades of use, they were covered up by tartan throws, but the room hadn't changed. Even now there was a comforting familiarity about it, although Joe's version of events was doing nothing to preserve my memories. 'Why would she have gone back to the old ways after all this time? Give me one good reason.'

Joe didn't hesitate, 'She thought she was cursed.'

It had been a long night and it was the last thing I expected to hear. I sat down and put my head in my hands and felt myself starting to hyperventilate. I knew Joe was an old man, but I didn't think his mind had gone.

'There's nothing wrong with my mind.'

I looked up, surprised. Joe was standing in front of me, red-faced and indignant. 'I've known you all your life. Sometimes I think I know you better than you know yourself, Peggy. I can almost see what you're thinking. You think 'Old Joe's gone daft', but it's not like that. Your mother told me she thought she was cursed. She kept saying she had only been allowed 50 years, and that her time was up. The Lady of Threepwood wouldn't let her forget.'

50 years. That was it. 50 years allowed. Finally, that elusive mental nugget fell into place. I had never for a moment thought she was being serious. Even she had played it down, dismissing it as a silly story when pressed but she never tired of telling it; and only ever to me. She said that after the incident the psychologists had seen to it that she didn't dwell on her so-called maudlin tendencies. But all that had achieved was to make her feel like an outsider. She clung to a veil of normality for the rest of her life, but now, looking back – perhaps it had all been nothing but a front? Had she really been seeing ghosts all these years? I had to know more.

'She said she had 50 years allowed?'

Joe was nodding, 'It was 50 years ago that she had what she called her incident. Her doubts had been gnawing away at her like a cancer. In the end she looked relieved.'

'I think you're exaggerating.' But Joe was shaking his head. 'Don't take my word for it Peggy, go up to her room and see for yourself.'

'See what?' Something didn't feel right.

'Just go up, and you'll see.'

Joe stood staring up, waiting for me to take his lead. With every word my nerves were growing, the anxiety tightening into a queasy knot in my stomach. If nothing else, a trip upstairs would give me time to think, allow me time away from Joe. He was acting strangely, and although it might just be grief, there were doubts gnawing at me as if I'd somehow missed the elephant in the room. He seemed to sense my mood and backed off.

'I'll wait here, if you don't mind. I've already seen more than enough for one day.'

I went out into the hall and started to climb the stairs, the ancient boards creaking under my weight. My mother's room was the door farthest from the top of the stairs at the end of the landing. It was closed. Standing to collect my thoughts, I plucked up the courage to go in and gently pushed the door ajar, half expecting to see my mother standing folding sheets. But of course she wasn't there. I was speechless when I walked back into a room that I no longer recognised. The wallpaper was covered in text. Scratched capitals and lower case all screamed a warning:

50 years allowed fifty years allowed RECKONING 50 YEARS ALLOWED! 50 years allowed fifty years allowed 50 YEARS ALLOWED 50 years allowed My reckoning comes 50 YEARS ALLOWED 50 years allowed fifty years allowed 50 YEARS ALLOWED! Reckoning 50 years allowed FIFY YEARS ALLOWED!

Fear the reckoning!

It seemed as if the words had engulfed my mother's final days. I thought I'd come to know her as a friend, but the more I learnt about her, the more I realised that she'd always been a stranger.

My world felt like it was falling apart, and with every new discovery came a slew of unanswered questions. Something told me that I wasn't going to sleep well tonight, so I went back downstairs, and fixed myself a drink.

Outside, a figure stirred on Cuff Hill, her journey nearly over.

10

The next week passed in a blur of red tape as we prepared for the cremation; it seemed my mother's lifetime obsession with fire hadn't been dampened by death. I laughed during the service but I think the minister mistook my mirth for grief. But I was OK. I felt calm, more so than I'd have thought.

After the funeral, John dropped me back at the farmhouse and drove home. Maggie and Martin hadn't come, they were still pretty young and we didn't feel it was the right way for them to remember their Gran. The service had been nice enough; a humanist affair with nods to the past. I found it difficult to relate to the person they were talking about. It seemed I'd learned so much these last few days that it had been like meeting my mother anew.

I'd talked for a long time that first night with Joe. He seemed convinced that my mother had rekindled her passion with the occult, or 'the old ways' as he called them. More than that, he said that my Mum had been convinced that she'd die on the day she actually did, and that she believed her reckoning was due. Joe said they'd spoken a lot in the last few weeks and that even with the sightings of the druid that she claimed to have seen through the course of her life, he still thought that she was happy.

But something didn't ring true. I still didn't understand what had changed for her, and I made up my mind to dig as deep as I could.

My first big surprise came back at the farmhouse. It was something I'd missed before, with my attention grabbed by the shocking graffiti. In her bedroom cupboard, I found a large, black metal box, warped and rusted with age. It was bound by three black bands which had strange symbols on the clasps. I went looking for Joe to ask him what he thought it was.

'It's for her ashes.'

My reaction was instant, 'There's no way she's going in that thing. Look at it, Joe, it's hideous.' I was horrified at the thought of just how far her mental health had deteriorated. I felt ashamed for not having noticed. Joe stood, quietly. He seemed to be expecting something from me, his next question apparently designed to make me accept the situation, rather than question my Mum's motives.

'But it's a box she held dear all her life, Peggy.' Joe was running his hand over the box admiring the craftsmanship, 'It came from the druids' graves. She said she wanted to return to nature; to go back to her roots.'

'Is that supposed to be a joke, Joe?' I was trying to lighten the mood but his mind was elsewhere.

'She told me everything she wanted. I can tell you now if you want, but the detail is in her will, plain for all to see. She wanted you to take care of her estate. She was quite definite about that.'

I didn't know what to say, so I thanked Joe for his help and asked if he wouldn't mind leaving. He looked hurt that I'd asked and I apologised but I really needed to collect my thoughts before going home to the family. To say he was reluctant to go was an understatement. He made great play about staying to make sure I was OK, but eventually, thank God, he relented and left. I listened for the car door to slam shut but it wasn't until I heard the gravel crackle under the power of his Land Rover that I allowed myself to relax.

Alone, at last. What a week.

I pulled up a chair and placed the black metal box on the kitchen table, and tried to think of the best course of action; follow my heart or honour my Mum?

In the end, of course, I carried out her wishes, although it had been a little embarrassing to see them through. Trying his best to disguise his disgust at my unorthodox container, the funeral director said the box was 'highly unusual' and tried to sell me a 'more upmarket' alternative. Eventually he let me have my way, muttering something he wouldn't repeat. Looking at the 'urn' as he insisted in calling Mum's box, I thought he might be right; there had always been something odd at the heart of our family.

Back at the farmhouse with John, we started going through some of Mum's things – old photos, books, and bills; all the detritus of life. The mundane nature of the everyday objects amplified the enormity of her loss. Knick-knacks and tat that I'd come to associate as part of the fabric of the house became isolated as specific mementoes of long gone days. A warped green jug that I'd tried to make at school still took pride of place on the kitchen window. Taken as a whole they combined to tell my own life story. It was depressing to realise that despite the everyday struggles that felt so important at the time, in the end it all came down to, well, just stuff.

As per Mum's will, the ashes were being delivered tomorrow. And that would be the start of another long day that would see her returned to the earth, her remains being cast around the base of the Rocking Stone.

31 October, Samhain

Joe joined us for breakfast and we ate in silence, waiting. In the end we didn't have to hang around for long and the newly filled box arrived back just after 10am. Thanking the undertaker I brought my mother's remains into the house and sat the box in the middle of the kitchen table. Not sure how to act, we all stood back and just looked at it. I still had a nagging feeling there was something I'd overlooked. The tension was unbearable.

'I'd like to get this over now, if you don't mind. Joe, are you sure you'll be OK to get up to the stone? Don't come just because I asked; only if you can manage?'

Joe drew himself up to his full height, his joints crackling with the effort but with an indignant look on his face all the same, 'I'm not for the knackers' yard yet, Peggy. I'll make it. For your mother's sake I'll get up that bloody hill, even if it kills me.'

John winced at the words and Joe knew he'd said the wrong thing, but I didn't mind. I knew what he meant. I acknowledged the gesture with a tight smile and we set off on my Mum's last journey, out into the hills that had dominated her life.

Striding off in silence the walk gave me a brief respite and time to think. The reading of the will had been a strange affair, with conditions placed around its execution. As Joe told me, the house, its contents and the wider estate were all signed over to me. As the only child this was no great surprise and in that sense, the will was unremarkable. However, my mother had stipulated that Joe carried her remains from the farmhouse to the Rocking Stone, where the box was to be handed over to me. I'd been instructed to order a special verdant green and pink garland to wear at her behest, and we were all asked to wear nothing but natural white fibre throughout the course of the day. Readings were to be made from a pagan book Joe called the grimoire. I don't mind admitting that I left the farm feeling pretty stupid, like a third-rate hippy, with my new white cotton gypsy skirt and my billowing blouse. Together the three of us trailed off along the flatlands with our heavy metal cargo.

Our first stop was at the druids' graves, the place where my Mum's troubles had begun. On cue, Joe dropped suddenly to his knees and burst into full voice, 'By the grace of the old Gods I gift you the life everlasting. To the otherworld this offering goes. With good heart I applaud the fate of the old and the new. Forever entwined, their journey starts today.'

In turn, I repeated the words as instructed and then took the lead for the climb to the Rocking Stone. John was finding it hard not to laugh and we both giggled as we snaked our way up the hill feeling ridiculous. John complained, 'Why couldn't she just have been buried; it would have been a lot easier on everyone.'

Joe cut in, angry and scathing, 'Quiet, you two. You know what your mother wanted.' We were being scolded like naughty school kids, but he was right to call us out, and we continued in silence.

About 20 minutes later we arrived. I hadn't been to the Rocking Stone for years, and I was shocked by how neglected the enclosure had become. The stone wall that circled the site had been levelled in places, with green moss now rampant across the dislodged stones. Several of the trees inside the enclosure were dead and rotting, while the area had been fenced off to cattle, allowing the grass to grow tall, so much so that we found it difficult at first to find the centre.

'There it is,' Joe was pointing ahead.

The grass was slippery underfoot with the brown mulch of decayed ferns framing a dangerous path to the Rocking Stone. Inside the circle, under the canopy of the birch trees, it felt much darker. Spindly branches clawed at the sky above, while the sun struggled to breach the thickening cloud. My nerves were growing and I was starting to feel a little sick, the easy jokes of the not long past were a distant memory. The Rocking Stone had been an important spot for my mother, but the folklore behind it had also been the idea which had tipped her over the edge. I was starting to regret having agreed to executing her final wishes and reading from her precious grimoire. But I knew there was no way that I could have reasonably refused. I just need to see it through. A voice behind reminded me that we'd nearly finished the ritual. Looking back I smiled at John. I noticed that Joe had fallen back to the perimeter wall, nodding his encouragement and willing me on. There was someone else not far behind him; a fourth figure in white. It must be another part of the ceremony, something we'd get to later. Remembering the order of the day I took my place by the stone.

The box had been set on top of the uneven oblong surface and I noticed that moss covered much of the Rocking Stone too, which was making it slippery. It took a while to balance the container. I'd relaxed a little in the last few moments. I was getting used to the dense woodland and breathed in the scent of my surroundings, the damp moss and foliage filling my lungs with memories of childhood walks. Gripped by a heavy nostalgia I took out the paper and started to read my mother's final words.

'I offer you this life, oh great Gods, for the journey to the otherworld. On my honour, trust, and sacred soul believe that this is offered freely. Oh great Gods and to the Lady of Threepwood, take this life for eternity.'

Guided by my own words I unfastened the branches which held down the lid and slowly opened the box, and tipped the ashes over the stone. What happened next was so sudden that it took me by surprise. I could hear John screaming in the background. Something's wrong. I was finding it really difficult to focus and around me the world blurred to a muddy fog as the ashes engulfed me. I saw a figure by my side. It was Joe. He whispered that my mother's 50 years had come at a price and that now was time of the reckoning. Looking down I saw something glint in his hand and then felt a sharp pain. I drew back my arm to try and move away. But Joe was gripping me roughly. Smearing me in my own blood he raised my arm and plunged my dripping hand into the ashes, screaming, 'I implore you mistress of the woods and masters of the rebel spirits to hear me now. I implore you to abandon your dwelling, in whatever part of the world you should be, to come to me now. I command you by the sacrifice I have made and as the great Gods command and by the power of the precious blood that has been spilled. Speak now spirit. Speak now.'

Around me was blackness. The world I knew had gone to flame. I waited and watched. The fire, which had sprung from nowhere, spread from the trees to the long grass. All around me the blaze raged hot and fast, forming a ring around the Rocking Stone. I could hear chants repeated again and again, for the great Gods and the lady of the woods. Then, gradually, the figures formed. First they were nothing more than flickers in the flames, and then slowly they appeared; a ring of hooded figures around the stone, life from the lifeless. In front of me was a woman in white and instinctively, somehow, I knew that it was the Lady of Threepwood, the bane of my mother's life.

Then she showed me her face. Such a shocking revelation. As she ventured through the scorching heat the druid's clothes lit up like a firework; the sparks starting a chain reaction which coursed through the circle as the landscape changed again. Her face remained, the only part seen as human flesh, and it was a face I knew. It was my mirror image. It was then that she spoke, for the first and only time. Her words would shatter my peace as she hissed her judgment.

'It is you that shall seek forever more, for we are one at last.' As the druid leaned closer, the ashes from the urn swirled up and around me, engulfing us both in an eternal darkness as we joined together. Joe and John had disappeared and I knew they were lost to me. The landscape was transformed as the low enclosure wall disappeared completely. All around me were standing stones, scorched black with fire. Beyond them an endless wood of tall slender birch trees. Coming round I noticed I had company. White robed figures circled around me, chanting as one. As the fire raged on I expected to feel the pain of the inferno that had consumed me. But there was nothing; no pain, no blistered skin or screams, no life or death, just the otherworld. The fiery wraith had gone but I finally knew her secret, why my mother had insisted that we return to the Rocking Stone. It was me that had stalked Threepwood, a journey that had lasted through the ages, and yet had only just begun. As the huddled mass of my new family gathered to worship the Lady of Threepwood for the first time a new song began in earnest. They brought forward a pristine, black metal box bound by three black bands with strange symbols on the clasps. My body turned to ash and yet my spirit endured. I watched in horror as my remains were sucked from me and deposited in the strange metal box and carried away.

I could only watch as the strange procession made its way down Cuff Hill to a newly dug grave. They buried the container and sealed my fate with a heavy stone slab.

From then on my life was not my own. Wandering, and bound to do their bidding, I swore an oath.

Be it the last thing I do, I will have vengeance.

The Rocking Stone

In Threepwood lies the Lady,
by the circle of the Rocking Stone.
Her warning comes from ages past,
cast out from the otherworld.

If you come to see her once, take heed,
she won't be far from home.
She shall not stop, she'll seek you out,
from the fire of the Rocking Stone.

Anon

The Cold, Black Sea

1988, Scotland

I slip under, choking on the water and brace myself for the worst. The force of the wave buffets me against the rocks. Gasping for breath, the rough seas suck me in, out and around the edges of the rocky outcrop.

A brief pause and I'm treading water. It's still light and I can see the beach, but all the time the undercurrent's pulling me further out into open water. My only hope of riding out the storm is to reach the rocks.

I'd plunged headfirst into the choppy sea full of confidence, but the tidal force and stormy conditions took me by surprise – and my bravado quickly disappeared, replaced by panic and fear. I keep as upright as possible, with my arms on the surface, desperately trying to stay afloat, but I know I'm fighting a losing battle. Large waves overwhelm me and I splutter out salt water. My arms are freezing and I'm losing energy; if I go under now I know I'll never come back.

I'm tired and starting to sink down into the depths. I hold my breath as the next surge pushes me back against the rocks. Arching my back to escape the onslaught of the jagged edges, I try frantically to grip on to something, anything, that might help me to safety.

The storm rages on, whipping the waves higher and faster until, for the briefest of moments, a dip appears close to the rocks. I plunge down before the next wave quickly throws me back to the surface, a strong swell casting me clear onto the rocks. I clutch around, trying to hang on, knowing another powerful wave is seconds away.

Looking up, I see a metal pole lodged at the summit of the rocks, a sign to warn others of danger, but a lifeline to me. My legs and hands are red raw and aching. In the fading light I stare blankly as blood drains off into the water. I hadn't even noticed that I'd been cut. There's no time to dwell on my injuries, though, and I use every ounce of strength to drag myself across the razor sharp barnacles, slipping on seaweed, and slowly slither my way to safety. Painfully, I edge up the last few feet and grasp the pole with both hands.

Eventually, the storm abates and the sea calms, the ebb and flow slowly sapping the last of my energy. Swimming back to shore is out of the question. I'm stranded. For hours I lie, shivering and contrite. What had I been thinking?

I was spotted the next morning by a beachcomber looking for flotsam and jetsam strewn out by the storm. In time, the lifeboat arrives and my rescuers prise me from the rocks, my hands locked fast around my dearest friend, that marvellous rusty metal pole. Looking back, I realise that I've been holding on ever since.

28 years later – Vancouver, Canada

The news hadn't been good but I thought I'd taken it well. I'd nodded and smiled, asked the right questions, then left. Just between you and me I'm not really great with doctors. The last time I gave blood I got weak at the knees, fell over and knocked myself out. And while I can laugh about it now, I'm struggling to conjure up any amusing anecdotes from my latest appointment. I leave the hospital and start the long walk home down a winding road. The sun splits through the canopy above, casting dancing shadows on the sidewalk. I smile; everything's going to be just fine.

Glasgow, Scotland

It's the centenary of the First World War and a series of events are underway to link living relatives with past winners of the Victoria Cross. In Glasgow, one of the memorials is giving officials a collective headache. Having drawn a blank from the usual channels, the City Council had cast its net far and wide in the search for connections to one of its own local heroes. Communications manager, Christine Bowman, had left no stone unturned. Christine knew that without her help, Charlie Balfour's story was in danger of being forgotten. She issued a call to arms:

National appeal launched for family of WW1 VC winner to step forward

100 years after a Scottish soldier was awarded the Victoria Cross for bravery during the Battle of the Somme in World War 1, a national search is underway to find surviving family. A special ceremony will take place in Glasgow on Thursday 26 October, to mark a hundred years to the day that the heroic acts took place.

As part of the national programme to mark the centenary of the war, commemorative paving stones are being laid across the UK to honour the 629 Victoria Crosses awarded during the conflict.

Charles Balfour VC was born on 10 October 1897 at Birch Cottage, Threepwood, before moving to Govan in Glasgow in 1901 to live with his extended family. During the war, Charles enlisted as part of the Highland Light Infantry, 15th Battalion in the British Expeditionary Force.

During the Battle of the Somme, the 15th were among the units which attacked the heavily fortified position near Gommecourt. Concrete strongholds, bristling with machine guns had repelled all previous assaults. Charles braved enemy lines to ensure new information made it back to command, before returning to and helping to capture the stonghold. For his actions that day Charles Balfour was awarded the Victoria Cross, with the citation stating that his courage and his example 'undoubtedly saved a critical situation'.

Charles Balfour was only 37 when he died on July 1, 1933 following an accident in Glasgow city centre.

Glasgow Provost, Susan McClachan, said that despite an extensive search no surviving family members had been found, "We're preparing a permanent memorial to mark Charles' valour in the Battle of the Somme, and we'd dearly love to have family members present at the ceremony, which is part of the national WW1 commemorations.

"Charles was born in Ayrshire but raised in Glasgow and I'd urge anyone with a personal connection to the Balfour family to get in touch to help remember a powerful story that will soon be set in stone for generations to come."

Anyone who thinks they may have a family connection is asked to contact the Civic Office at Glasgow Council on tel: 0141 559 3339, or email: provost@glasgow.gov.uk

Vancouver

Inoperable. That's how they'd described my cancer. It took a while to sink in but when they told me I was terminal I was more relieved than anything else. I'd been feeling ill for a while. Not in agonising pain or anything like that, but definitely a sub-par version of myself. I exercise a lot and it had been getting harder to keep up the pace. My running times had been getting slower and I'd noticed my energy levels had dropped off along with my appetite. Worst of all, though, were the headaches. They started as a throbbing pulse, which I'd put down to too much screen time. I'm a graphic designer to trade and long days in front of a monitor are my bread and butter. I read a lot too, so I just thought I'd been overdoing it.

The first serious warning sign came in the most innocuous of places; the swimming pool. I was in the middle of my fourteenth length when a sharp shooting pain coursed through my body. The next I knew I was being revived at the side of the pool; they said I'd sunk to the bottom.

So, things had progressed quite quickly and when the call came to ask me back to Scotland I knew I was running out of time. Like I said earlier, on diagnosis day I left the hospital, the sun was shining and I smiled; there were worse ways for it to end. I booked my flights and phoned my brother.

By the end of the week I'd be home for the first time in nearly thirty years. I knew that not everyone would be pleased to see me.

Glasgow

It had been a slow day in the newsroom and Sandy Stirrit skimmed the press release without giving it too much thought. The story was no great shakes; a photo opportunity from a council trying to track down relatives of a war hero. The release said the man was being honoured with a plaque to commemorate the 100th anniversary of the Battle of the Somme. The Council hadn't been able to track down any surviving members of the family and they were asking for help. Sandy noticed there was a link which clicked through to a number of grainy period pictures. The typically sensational bio suggested Charles Balfour had kept communications channels open single-handedly, helping to gain ground on the day. It said his luck hadn't lasted and Charles died in Glasgow a few years later. The reporter in him knew there was more than enough human interest for a decent feature.

Hero's return

Christine Bowman's media campaign had been a big success. Scrolling through the email chain she knew she'd found the perfect person to invite to the WW1 commemoration. In the end her call for help had been answered from Canada. Maggie Balfour was Charles Balfour's third cousin and Christine had been thrilled when Maggie had agreed to be their guest of honour. The council paid for the flight and Christine was now finalising arrangements for Maggie to attend the ceremony in two days' time. Christine didn't know it then, but it was going to be a day to remember.

Vancouver International Airport

I approached the plane with mixed emotions. Turning on the air stair, I took a last look at my adopted home and sighed. There's nothing here for me now. Boarding the cabin, the rush of air from the vents competes with the muffled roar of the jet engines outside. I shuffle down the aisle looking for my seat.

Later, the clink of plastic and cans from cabin crew collecting rubbish is starting to get on my nerves and even the tinny rasp of nearby earphones is driving me nuts. I glance across at my neighbour. He's watching a disaster movie and laughing loudly. I've never understood why people think they can't be heard. There are still four hours to go before we land. The on-board screen tells me that we're cruising at 35,000 feet, and as we hurtle back to the UK I wonder what kind of welcome I'll get.

I need a distraction and log on to the Wi-Fi. As I sit, mulling over the past, my phone lights up with my brother's face on screen. He's waiting for me in Scotland. I swipe the bar and take the call.

'Hey Martin, how's it going?'

It's a bad line and the picture phases in and out, but I can hear his voice loud and clear, 'It's been so long, Maggie, I didn't think you'd ever come back.'

It's fair to say we've always had a fairly difficult relationship and we haven't spoken much since I'd upped sticks and moved to Canada in the mid-nineties. I'd always found him a little too needy. Everything changed in that doctor's surgery, though, and the time had come to make my peace.

I tried to listen to what Martin was saying but my neighbour had turned up the volume on his earphones and all I could hear was an alarm on the soundtrack. On his screen a helicopter billowed smoke and circled back to Earth. I don't know if it was the suggestion of falling or just my body telling me to take more heed but a searing pain courses through my stomach. It hits home hard, like a punch, and I wince. Doubling over, my head lands on the seat in front. Dammit if I'll ever remember to take my pills at the right time. I realise that I've forgotten about Martin and pick up the phone again, 'I'm going to have to call you back, there's turbulence right now.' I paw at the phone trying to kill the line but I can still see my brother's outline on the handset. It's as if he's trying to look behind me, to see what's going on. The old irritations rise again and I snap, releasing the tension I'd felt these last few hours, 'For God's sake just leave me alone. We'll speak later.' I push the handset down the back of the magazine holder, crushing the in-flight magazine. Peace at last.

I'm trying to focus on my breathing when I realise I've got company. The tinny rasp has gotten louder and when I turn I see my neighbour has taken his earpiece out. He's staring at me, holding his headphones in one hand while the film continues, momentarily unwatched. One of the cabin crew is standing beside him, clutching a swaying black bin bag, stuffed full with plastic and card. She looks a bit officious, with her small military style cap and uniform. I can taste bile at the top of my throat, which is doing nothing to improve my mood. The stewardess is staring at me with a slightly confused look.

'Is everything OK, madam?'

Her face ripples in the light and I notice her nose move almost imperceptibly as the early sun casts shadows through the plane.

'I was just talking to my brother.'

The air hostess nods and glances at my neighbour, 'Is this your brother, madam?'

I don't understand and just shake my head. I ask her for water and she leaves. I watch her talking to colleagues at the other end of the plane, by the supply area. They're all looking up and my heart starts to race. I put my hand under the chair and drag out my bag. My drugs are set out in compartments, so I take the pills and swallow. By the time the attendant comes back with the glass I'm crying and feel totally lost. The doctors had told me that flying at altitude wouldn't be a good idea and they'd been right. I gripped the armrest tightly and tried to steady my racing heart. This is going to be a long journey.

***

Outside, we fly over endless ocean, its flow ever changing. Vast cargo ships cut through high seas, ferrying goods across the Atlantic to mail order warehouses; their epic journeys unappreciated by lazy shoppers in cosy homes. Swimmers stab at the edges, as the tide washes out from golden shores. Waves pulse for hundreds of miles, creating power enough to light up cities and sweep them away in equal measure. Like a speck in the sky, my plane wisely keeps its distance from the tempest below. As we soar homeward, I search my mind for answers to the same old questions, but as usual draw a blank. I hope that my brother can throw me the lifeline I so desperately need.

Vancouver

Darcie Fen had been pacing her apartment for the best part of an hour, worried sick about her friend. Maggie was never late and Darcie hadn't had so much as a text from her. It was completely out of character. Darcie pulled back the blinds and looked out. A car was pulling up at the top of the street and for a second her hopes were raised, but it u-turned and left. With a sharp intake of breath, Darcie phoned Maggie's landline and mobile again, but both rang out. Darcie had been getting worried about Maggie's behaviour in recent weeks. Her friend would jump at the slightest sound and often just stare into space. Today, Darcie was sure something was wrong. She grabbed her car keys from the hall table and left; she needed to know Maggie was OK. In the car she flicked on the radio and crunched through the gears. On the radio, a golden oldie wonders if there's life on Mars.

Descent

I've never been a great flier and it hadn't been a great flight. I was standing in the aisle when the plane started its juddering descent. A trolley dolly grabbed my arm and told me to sit down. No chance. I feel sicker than ever. I need my pills. I wrestle free from my high-flying nemesis and pull the catch on the overhead baggage, but that's as far as I get. Jackets tumble down and the air stewardess pulls me back, points at the seatbelt sign, and tells me to sit. I try in vain to reason with her but she doesn't want to know.

Looking out through the clouds, the window's warped with condensation and the ground looms ever closer. I feel certain that I'll die before we land; but of course I don't, there's no respite.

The airport isn't much better. On the runway I hastily neck my medication; the heat of the engine burning the icy air, leaving vapour trailing skywards. I stand for a moment, staring at the hazy patterns as my pills race south to work their magic.

Looking back at the plane, the mist above reveals unexpected shapes; like the animals I saw in clouds as a child. The thought vanishes when a hand on my elbow drags me back to reality. It's an older man wearing thick black glasses, an orange hat and a black rucksack. I take an immediate dislike to him.

'Are you OK?' He asks. He's looking behind me and, turning, I see his family hanging back; his wife and two blonde kids looking on awkwardly. I hurry off, not wanting to talk. Glancing back he's shaking his head in an 'I know but what can I do' kind of way that really pisses me off. Behind him the misty shapes above the plane turn black. I turn and tell him to mind his own bloody business. He seems surprised, but I'm in no mood to be patronised. I stride off past his family and smile; I hear them arguing in my wake. It's good to be back.

Vancouver

Darcie Fen knocked on Maggie's door but got no reply. Frustrated, she pressed the buzzer hard and let it ring. After waiting a few seconds, she presses her ear to the door and listens. Silence. Crouching down to peer through the letter box she is shocked by the state of the apartment. Maggie is the tidiest person she knows. Darcie often complained about having to take her shoes off as soon as she crossed the threshhold. Maggie fretted about marks on her carpet – but the image Darcie had of her neat freak friend didn't fit with what she saw. In the hallway a mug was upended on the floor, a thick black coffee stain spreading out. Darcie couldn't see too far inside, but there was a smell of rot inside and no sign of life. Darcie had last seen her less than a week ago but the place looked abandoned.

Darcie was getting more worried by the minute. She went round to the back and peered through the windows. It looked like they had been deliberately caked with dirt. She could see nothing inside. It seemed she may not have known her friend as well as she'd thought. Darcie took out her phone and called the Police.

Glasgow International Airport

I was born in Scotland but there's nowhere there I can really call home. I do have friends from the old days, though, and I decided to call on the kindness of my oldest pal. I look at my watch. It had taken longer than expected to find a taxi at the airport. There had been a long queue of soldiers waiting at the front of the airport, all dressed in old fashioned uniforms. I assumed it must be something to do with the centenary commemorations for the war. If they're hoping to make a splash they must be feeling pretty underwhelmed; a typical city reaction dictated that no-one paid them much notice. Children skipped and pointed, but the adults kept about their business – checking for cash and passports, patting down pockets and bags as they made their way to security. I watch for a while. The men are sitting on kit bags singing 'Pack up your troubles'. I think about great uncle Charlie, spellbound, and time seems to slip away. I notice that one of the soldiers, a man with an angular face and sharp nose, is watching me. I smile and he turns away. Not long after, the singing stops and the men disperse back through the terminal. I feel sad that it's over and ask a women in the queue what she thinks of it all. She just looks at me and smiles, before moving off down the side of the building. I go looking for a taxi.

About ten minutes later I'm on the motorway heading south. I try to chat with the driver but I can't hear what he's saying over the din of the radio which is making me mad. It's an 80s station playing far too loud and the music is making my head hurt. At the same time he's trying to strike up small talk and while I can see his lips moving in the mirror, I can't make out what he's saying. I must have been shouting because he pulls over onto the hard shoulder. The music stops abruptly and he asks if I want to travel or not? I say yes, but he looks so angry. I realise what's wrong. Raking through my bag I take out the small plastic container and hold the blue tablets in the palm of my hand. Have I already taken too many? I curse myself for forgetting and I feel the pills grate on the edge of my throat as I swallow them down regardless. Pulling away from the hard shoulder the taxi gathers speed and we continue our journey. I check the time. I'll be at Gillian's house in about 15 minutes. It'll be great to see her again.

***

Approaching Gillian's place, it's much the same as I remembered; a small, dismal cottage on the outskirts of town. The last time I was here it was quite run down, with paint flaking from the walls, but it was gleaming white today and had scrubbed up about as well as it could. The rose garden was out of season and bare. The house had been on the main drag at one time but they'd built a new road north which had cut the cottage off. With no through traffic the single track road was empty and full of potholes. The taxi bumps along at a snail's pace before trundling to a halt. The driver takes my money, opens the trunk and leaves my luggage on the side of the road, before walking off muttering something about suspension. I look back at the cottage and see a whisper of smoke coming from the chimney. Someone's home. I knock on the door and wait.

Inside, someone's moving about, but no-one comes to the door. I knock again and bend over to peer through the letter box, 'Gillian are you in there? It's me, Maggie.'

Something catches my eye and glancing right I see the curtain move. I'm being watched. It seems that Gillian's feeling a bit anxious about seeing me. I wonder if I should have phoned ahead to let her know exactly when I'd arrive. But it was Gillian; she won't mind.

In the distance there's a dull roar, like thunder. When I look up a plane cuts a distant shadow but there's not a cloud in the sky. My distraction is short-lived and I twist round when the door opens. The frame shudders as the chain inside holds fast. A face looks out at me through the narrow opening.

'Who's there?'

'Hi Gillian, it's me, Maggie.' I can see the side of her face but she doesn't say anything and seems to be waiting for me to keep talking, so I fill the void and ramble on. 'I'm just off the plane and I told you to expect a visit. Surely you've got the time to say hi to an old pal?'

A jangled scrape of metal fills the air, as Gillian removes the security chain to finally reveal herself. She's wearing jeans and an old blue jumper. Her hair has greyed out a bit and she's bigger than I remember, but I'd have recognised her anywhere. I smile; 'I've come back.'

'But it's been…'

I didn't need to count, it had been 28 years since we'd last seen each other. She opens the door and lets me in and I hug her like a long lost sister. The warmth of the memory was making me well up. We've got a lot of catching up to do.

Vancouver

Darcie Fen felt sick. The police had taken about an hour to arrive and in the end they didn't stay long. Darcie said that she was worried, that this was all completely out of character for Maggie. The cop was a young guy who tried his best to hide his impatience as Darcie made her case to report a missing person.

'I was here two days ago and the place was immaculate. Just look at the mess. Maggie wouldn't do something like this. I'm worried about her,' said Darcie. The cop nodded but didn't reply, prompting Darcie to continue. 'It's just not like her to take off,' she turned and pointed at the ground floor apartment, 'just look at those windows, does that look normal to you?'

Darcie strode off across the lawn to point at the glass, which was smeared and misty from dried earth. 'Why would she do this?' The nodding cop kept up his momentum. 'Damnit, why aren't you going to do anything? Don't you even care – what needs to happen for this to spike your ass into actually doing something?' Darcie stopped abruptly when she realised she'd been shouting. The cop's partner had been looking around the yard. He stopped when Darcie raised her voice. She watched his hand go to his baton and suddenly felt very vulnerable. 'I'm sorry, I shouldn't have lost my temper, it's just – well, she's my friend and I don't know what to do.'

The cop sighed and apologised. He said the records didn't show her as missing and that her name wasn't showing up on any of the city hospital records. He said they'd log the complaint and try to phone Maggie when they could. Try not to worry, he said. She'll show up.

Darcie left them in the yard and went back to her car. She felt a bit light-headed. None of this felt right.

What she didn't know then was that she'd never see Maggie again.

Glasgow, newsroom

Scrolling through the newsroom database Sandy Stirrit was trying to remember what it was about the guest of honour that felt so familiar, but so far he'd drawn a blank. He knew the face from somewhere, though, he was sure of it. Sandy looked again at the picture that he'd been sent with the follow-up press release. The council had tracked down one of the family members in Canada. The image of Maggie Balfour was obviously quite old. The styles looked to be from the late 80s. The pastel blouse and jeans looked so out of time.

He smiled at a memory from his own past, but the work wouldn't wait and he ploughed on. A trawl for Charles Balfour was next on the list. There were a lot of websites with references to his war hero days, regimental accounts and the like, but not much about his later life. The only thing that showed up was the fact that he'd died in the city centre after being hit by a tram.

Sandy scratched his head; he was sure he'd missed something. The memorial service was taking place later that week. Sandy decided that he'd use the time to do more homework before he met with Maggie face-to-face.

Gillian Casselly

Gillian had been dreading meeting Maggie from the moment that she'd phoned. It was true that they had been great friends as kids, but that had all changed after the scandal. When she'd disappeared off to Canada, Gillian had never really expected to see Maggie again, but earlier that day the phone rang, quite out of the blue, and here she was.

Gillian just stared at her and the memories came flooding back. The shock, the questions, the media attention and all that stress. And for what? In the end what could they prove; absolutely nothing. It had been a long time since she'd thought about any of it but the force of confronting it so suddenly made her feel physically sick.

Reunited

I hadn't seen Gillian in such a long time. When the door opened she was fighting back tears and trembling. She seemed pretty overwhelmed by my arrival so I drop my bags, cross the threshold and hug her hard. She tries to pull away but I hold her tight. I'm not sure how long we stand like that until she finally breaks the silence.

'I suppose you'd better come in Maggie.'

I nod and move past her and make my way to the living room. I hear her outside gathering my bags and I watch from the front window as she struggles with the weight. Then, when the door clicks shut I hear her muttering under her breath and by the time she comes back I'm already getting annoyed.

'Aren't you going to offer me a cup of tea? I've been travelling all day.' She was just staring at me with her jaw slightly open. I was amazed at how little she'd changed; all her curious quirks were slowly revealing themselves. I breathe in deeply and savour the musty smell of the house. Gillian nods and leaves the room. I creep over and listen at the door until I hear water running in the kitchen, and pull back when my phone starts to ring. It's my brother again.

'Twice in one day. I feel honoured, Martin. It's not really a good time, though, I'm at Gillian's. Can I phone you back?' There's no sound at the other end for a few seconds, save for static. The handset crackles and then his voice comes through, weak at first, then it's like he's standing right beside me.

'What are you doing there, sis? Don't you think it's time to put an end to all the nonsense once and for all?'

'I don't know what you mean.' I'm not going to play his game. Ever since we'd been children he'd tried to manipulate me, played my parents off against each other to get his own way. That was a lifetime ago. He didn't have any power over me now. My attention's distracted by what sounds like an engine spluttering into life. I look outside, but there's nothing there and the noise stops almost as soon as it had started. I pull at my sweater, suddenly feeling very hot. Looking up the road I see the tarmac shimmering in the sunshine. The haze reminds me what I'd come here to do.

Newsroom

Sandy Stirrit had been in the library archives for a couple of hours. He was starting to piece together an intriguing family history. The internet search for Charlie Balfour had thrown up a lot of service-related tales of derring-do and it seemed reasonable to Sandy that he'd be honoured on the 100th anniversary of the Somme. There was very little about Charlie Balfour the man. Sandy read that Charlie had worked for the Corporation's Trams in Glasgow before the war, but with that network long gone there were few files left to give the reporter much to follow up. Sandy considered what he'd been able to find out. Charlie showed up on the 1921 census as unemployed and living in a Gorbals tenement. He'd been unmarried then. The only other information suggested that he'd died before his time. Tracing his family back to the previous census showed he had been living with his family in Ayrshire before leaving for a life in the city with his mother. It seemed he'd come from a broken home. Another mystery.

And then there was Maggie Balfour, his distant relative. It was then that the penny finally dropped. It was the more recent history that really hooked Sandy's interest. It had been one of the great unsolved mysteries. He wondered if, after all these years, he could be the one to uncover what had really happened.

Gillian Casselly

Gillian could hear Maggie talking loudly in the living room and wondered who she was speaking to. It would still be early in Canada and she wasn't aware of anyone else that Maggie was still in touch with in the UK. Gillian didn't want to go back through until after the call was over. If nothing else it would give her time to think. Looking longingly at the back door, Gillian felt the urge to run, but seconds later cursed her indecision. Gillian bit her lip and tried to think. Raking through the cutlery drawer she prised out a small utility knife and put it up the sleeve of her jumper. I won't be bullied by her again, she thought. By now, the tea was starting to get cold and although Maggie was still talking, Gillian decided to take matters into her own hands. She placed two mugs on a small, round floral-patterned tray and arranged some biscuits on a plate.

The mugs slid and clinked on the tray as she crept out across the hall. In the living room the noise stopped; the door swung open and Maggie glared out at her.

***

I glared out at Gillian and watched her twitch, with tea splashing across her tatty old tray. 'Just what do you think you're doing?' I'd startled Gillian but she quickly regained her composure. Gillian asks who I've been talking to, but I just stare at her and gesture to the nearest chair.

We sit for a while, holding the warm mugs, drinking in silence. On the TV there's footage of Margaret Thatcher and the miners strike. I can't understand the apparently endless appetite for nostalgia. My motto is 'Live for the moment', so I pick up the remote control and turn down the volume. Gillian is sitting, slack-jawed and looking at me apologetically.

'What's wrong with you?' I ask. 'How do you think we're going to be able to talk with all this noise?' Gillian raises her hand to point at the TV. She keeps repeating the same word 'But, but, but—'

'—but nothing, just try and focus. We've a lot to talk about.'

Silence again and more strained, distant looks. Eventually Gillian plucks up the courage to speak.

'Is this something to do with your family?'

I don't flinch, I'd been expecting it, 'What do you mean?'

'I know they asked you back for the World War One thing, but it's been more than thirty years since it all happened.' I knew what she was getting at. It had been 34 years, four months and three days since my family vanished and my life had been transformed for the worse.

'That's all in the past. You were there at the time. I don't need to go through all that again.'

'But you changed after that.'

'Who wouldn't?'

'But it's never really been resolved.'

'They're all gone. You know that. Sometimes people don't get found.'

'And that's it? That's what you've learned after all this time? Surely there must be part of you that wants to know what happened?'

I was starting to feel hot again; hot and sick. The garish striped wallpaper warps in the light, the strong beams from the slatted blinds sears off silver strips and bounces back to blind me. My stomach lurches and I feel bile start to rise. This isn't a good time or place for one of my weak moments. My phone starts to ring again and I'm vaguely aware of a voice in the background.

I can see it it's my brother. I need to speak to him. I'm glad he hasn't forgotten to phone back. Doubled-up, I wait for the nausea to pass, but the shooting pain leaves me paralysed on the floor. From the corner of my eye I briefly see Martin's face, before the pale green screen flickers to black.

Newsroom

Sandy Stirrit needed background. His research uncovered some old letters of Charlie's from his time at the Somme, one of which mentioned hallucinations. Sandy wondered if Charlie had been suffering from shell shock. The treatment for that had been death by firing squad, but this soldier had survived – even if he had turned to drink to cope. Sandy made a mental note to add in some of the detail to his feature.

Thumbing through the rest of his notes there was all the drama with Maggie's family. The Balfour kids had been split up after their parents disappeared in the early 80s. Maggie and Martin had been left with friends while their mother and father scattered ashes at a family funeral. What came later was almost as bad and Sandy couldn't help but pity the children. The next few years had been particularly rough for them.

Sandy printed out a copy of the report about the later scandal. He spent a long time studying the picture showing the police cordon round the beach. Tomorrow he would find out more.

Gillian Casselly

Gillian tried to help Maggie up off the floor but she pushed back, red faced, and shouted, 'Get your hands off me. I need to speak to Martin.'

Gillan backed off, 'Maggie, we need to talk this through.'

Maggie had found her feet again and grabbed a heavy glass ash tray from the window sill, clutching the side and brandishing it like a weapon, threatening her friend, 'You can go to hell, Gillian. You were no bloody use to me back then and it looks like nothing's changed!'

The transformation in Maggie was complete and Gillian raised her hands defensively and pushed back to try and pacify her friend, 'It's alright, I'm not here to judge you,' Gillian had drawn the knife she'd concealed and was warily prodding it into thin air, hoping to deter her friend from getting too close. 'Maybe you need to speak to someone who can help, I'm not sure I—'

She was interrupted mid-flow when Maggie launched the ashtray at her across the room. Gillian ducked and it smashed off the back wall.

'I'm quite sure you can't help, Gillian.' Maggie was red with rage, her breathing was fast and rough. She turned and left, slamming the door behind her.

Gillian watched her friend outside from the safety of her living room. The encounter had left her mentally exhausted, while an adrenaline rush was coursing through her shaking body. Maggie was speaking to someone on the phone and Gillian only caught fragments of the conversation. A few moments later Maggie was gone, having left all of her things in the hall. As Gillian eyed the cases with a sinking feeling, she prayed that they'd never meet again.

Retreat

I checked-in to the nearest hotel. It's a shabby 10-room affair in a drive-through town, but it gives me shelter and a place to think. I paw at the plastic container for what feels like the 100th time today. The bloody pills are insufferable but they're all I've got to take the edge off the pain. I take three more and swallow, the cold water easing the tablets home. I sit on the bed for a while, my heavy breathing signposting a potential panic attack. I'm distracted by the gentle buzz of my mobile and answer on the third ring to greet Martin, 'You promise you'll come tomorrow?' I ask. There's a sigh at the end of the line.

'I'll be there sis, you can bet your life on it.'

I hang up, relieved. Now, more than ever, I need to feel grounded. I spend the night trying to remember, but it's useless, too much has happened. Eventually, I lie down and try to sleep. All I can think of are my many mistakes.

Headland Wood

On the day of the ceremony I wake up with a splitting headache and decide to make my own way to Headland Wood. The council have planned their big reveal for great uncle Charlie in a remembrance park not far from where I'm staying. Charlie Balfour was born near here too. The officials said it was a fitting place for a lasting reminder of his wartime exploits. That's what they'd said anyway. I knew from the organisers' reaction that people get awfully excited about this kind of thing. I'd agreed at the time, but the more I think about it, the more uneasy it makes me feel. Charlie had been honoured for keeping communication lines open during the war. They said he had saved lives, but with tens of thousands of men lost during the battle his contribution was just a drop in the ocean. How many people had to die for him to land the dubious honour of being labelled a hero?

I arrive by foot and stop at the estate's imposing wrought iron gates. They're an ornate affair, with carved figures of stags, birds and assorted beasts scrolled across the sandstone columns which held them in place. The winter solstice isn't far off and it feels cold. Overhead, just a few leaves cling to the rickety web of branches. I'd come early to give myself time to prepare. Having lived in a busy city for so long I was finding the stillness of home quite unsettling, a feeling amplified in this isolated woodland.

I was meant to meet them at Grahamston House in the heart of the woodland. It turns out that it's a long walk. A single lane winds through the dense forest, with a slight rain drizzling down on me in spits and spots. There's distant noise; occasional cracks that make me jump, while animals dart off and birds hop from branch to branch. My heart's beating fast from the exercise and I wonder if I should have accepted the invitation of an escort from County Hall after all. A new noise stops me dead in my tracks. It sounds like drums. A slow rhythmic military beat, which fades in the breeze. I pick up my pace.

The road spills downhill to reveal the decayed structure of Grahamston House a mile or so away. It had been gutted by fire a long time ago, with only a small part restored. Bright light shines through empty windows giving the illusion of life. I imagine the house must still be in use after all – but the nearer I get the more I realise my mistake.

Squinting against the early sunlight I spot a few huddled figures and a number of official looking cars.

***

The Provost had been looking at her watch every few minutes, 'You're sure this woman is definitely coming?'

Christine Bowman nodded again and told her the woman had a name, 'Maggie Balfour said she'd be here well before time, and we still have an hour to go.'

The Provost tutted. 'I don't know why you couldn't have insisted she meet us at County Hall. It would have made life so much easier.'

Christine, trying not to rise to the bait, scanned the horizon for signs of life, anything to shut the Provost up, 'I think I can see her now.' Christine pointed up the road towards the tree line, 'There's someone coming down the hill. Can you see?' She waved at the distant figure but got no response.

***

Oh my God they're waving. I suddenly feel the need to speed up. The group's obviously impatient to meet me. As I draw nearer I see a group of around 15 people waiting in a huddle. The gaggle of suits around a woman dressed in a red, ermine-collared robe make for a strange welcome party. Further back, a number of men and women are dressed in WW1 military costumes, rifles and all, just like the group I'd seen at the airport. One of them is staring directly at me, underlining my sense of déjà vu. Before I have time to give it any more thought the red robed figure breaks the ice with a practiced grin and extends a hand. It was the start of what would prove to be a difficult day.

When we arrive at the clearing they show me Charlie's plaque. It was covered by a Union Flag, and had been embedded in a fallen tree trunk in the middle of a sculpture park.

'We're really proud of our work here,' the Provost said, 'Not so long ago this whole area was completely overgrown,' she gestures broadly, 'but as you can see, we've cut it all away and started installing a series of wooden statues. You'll see everyone's contribution to the Great War included here.' I nod while the Provost keeps talking, 'Over there you can see our machine gun outpost, while in the distance is our most elaborate effort, a full sized biplane.'

I smile because it seems to be what she wants but I'm distracted. The people in costume are taking up their places around the forest, lining the way for the guests due in a few minutes time. The actors are straightening helmets, adjusting tunics, while one of them near to the biplane is inspecting his rifle. I don't like guns and the militarised barren landscape is doing nothing to settle my nerves.

'Why have you given your actors real guns?' I said to no-one in particular. I walk a few steps ahead of the group and glance back. They're all watching me with a marked curiosity. I'm distracted when the nausea takes hold again; it seems to be eating away at me a little bit more each day. I barely heard her response.

'No-one here has any real guns,' said the Provost.

'What about that man over there?' I look ahead and point. The man near the biplane has lifted his rifle and to my horror he's aiming straight at me.

It was as if I'd been pulled into a fog. The dreich daylight dims and the burble of the wood gives way to a cacophony of noise and a full blown warzone. The bullets buzz like bees, the barrage turns the sky black, with men reduced to a puff of crimson in the blink of an eye. Earth churns, while fragments of wood splinter past me at speed. Suddenly I'm afraid. Explosions rage all around. Soldiers run, screaming loudly, some stopping to fire-off shots, while craters open up under shell fire. Yet for all the drama, I feel detached, as if none of it is real.

In the distance the soldier I'd seen before is standing absolutely still. He aims with the calmness of a sniper, his rifle is raised and I'm in his sights. Through the din I hear a crack. I sense the bullet more than see it and the world crashes quickly into slow motion. On instinct I throw myself to the ground, the soft muddy track helping to cushion the blow. Winded, I push myself back up onto my knees to be greeted by silence. From behind, strong arms lift me up and a voice asks if I'm OK? I ask myself the same question but my thoughts are frazzled by my latest vision. I don't know what's happening to me.

***

Caked in mud they take me to a clearing, away from the main site, and ask me to sit down and 'collect myself', whatever that means. It had all seemed so real but yet I knew it couldn't have been. With every passing day I'm losing confidence in my senses. In the last few weeks I'd experienced a number of minor visions and ripples in sight, but I'd been told to expect these as side-effects of the drugs – but this had been vivid, so vivid.

The woodland is filling up with spectators and more than a few journalists. There is little I can do now to avoid making a public appearance. The council people hand me a pack with information about the day and a list of things they want me to say. I skim it over but struggle to take it all in. Today was meant to be about Charlie Balfour, but he's fast becoming a sideshow, with yours truly now the star attraction.

I reach into my long black trench coat and pull out one of the only pictures I have of Charlie. The photo was taken during the war, and showed a young Charlie with no smile or glimmer in his eyes, just a man nervous about going off to war. He had the family nose; the long, thin pointed end had plagued the Balfours for years, but it was the one thing that helped me to really connect with him, we looked so alike. I sit and hold the print for ages. A hand on my shoulder brings me back to the here and now. A woman in a suit tells me that things are about to get underway, so I pick myself up and get on with it.

Standing there, among the great and the good, I feel like a complete imposter. They'd only asked me to come because no-one else was available. I'll bet they wished they hadn't bothered now. Martin said he didn't want to play an active role in the event but he'd promised to turn up. True to form, though, he's nowhere to be seen.

I hear my name called and step forward, say the words I'd memorised while gazing vacantly at the tree line. Out of the corner of my eye I see the costumed actors stand at attention with their heads bowed. My eyes scan the crowd before resting on one man who looks up and catches my glance. He's familiar, somehow, and at first I can't place him. I continue my speech on auto-pilot, but keep looking back to the mysterious spectator. He's a young man with a long, thin pointed nose. I gasp when it dawns on me. It's like looking into a mirror. It can't be, though, but there's no mistaking the face from the picture. It seemed as if Charlie was staring right back at me and for a few seconds I completely lose my way, stumbling my speech to silence. This cannot be happening. It can't be real. He looks at me like he knows my darkest secret – the one thing I haven't dared tell to a living soul. I can't look away as he raises his rifle, aims directly at me and fires.

'No Charlie, no,' I scream. My head wants this to be another side-effect; another drug addled hallucination. I close my eyes and wait for the release of the bullet. I wait and wait but it doesn't come. There's a murmur of voices and when I open my eyes a sea of faces are staring back at me, intently focused. It's happened again.

At the back of the crowd I see that Martin has finally arrived, but he looks annoyed. He's shaking his head and quickly turns away. Not this time, Martin, please. I need you. But it's too late; he's gone.

Someone asks if I want to continue but I can't stay now. I tell the crowd the experience has been too much, that I haven't been well, and I leave.

Walking back through the woods alone a panic starts to build. I no longer feel in control and my senses are working overtime as I try to keep myself on an even keel. In the foliage all around me the rustling of animals continues but it's amplified by a hiss of distant voices, all trying to make themselves heard.

The spell's broken when someone calls my name and I turn back. One of the reporters is coming my way, waving his arms to try and get my attention. I make up my mind, turn and run as fast as I can.

What had started as a nostalgic trip home was fast turning into a living nightmare.

Threepwood

I had no choice but to put Headlands Wood behind me and turn my attention to the real reason I'd come home. I hadn't been back at Threepwood Farm since the 80s, but navigating the winding road was bringing it all back. Rotting grass and barren hedgerows framed the way and the landscape welcomed me like a long-lost friend. It was still rugged too and my rental car's tiny engine was struggling to match the challenge of Threepwood Hill and stalled near the summit. At the same time and the radio reception cut out, leaving me listening to the fuzz of white noise.

After a pause I try to get going and after three attempts the engine turns over and rasps back to life. I press my foot down hard on the accelerator. The wheels strain against the handbrake like dogs on a leash. I push the lever down and head off over the brow of the hill.

I see the farm well before I arrive; its distinctive silhouette made for a stark contrast to the rugged, pine-topped hills behind. The old homestead sat uphill from the reservoir and the water glistened in the autumn sun. I smile at thoughts of summer days and walks to the Rocking Stone. I'm emotional to be back. I'm finding it hard to reconcile the warmth of my past against the harsh reality of a life defined by cancer.

Lost in my journey down memory lane I somehow miss the turn-off and screech to a halt. I don't understand. I've been here a hundred times. I know the road like the back of my hand. I can see the farm's chimney pots over a distant hedge, but the access road had become overgrown. I park in a lay-by and walk.

Eventually I find it. The driveway's been fenced-off and abandoned. Years of growth and fairly mature trees have grown up unchallenged, with tall grass and gorse helping to obscure the way in. I stop for a second as a wave of pain takes hold, grabbing my sides in a vain effort to stay focused. I take more pills, my dry throat resisting this latest attempt at self-medication.

I catch my breath and carry on. Climbing over the rusted gate is a real effort. I stumble on the wavering metal barrier, falling over to the other side. A small bush helps to cushion my fall, but cuts me at the same time. I find myself lying in a shallow puddle.

Looking around it's sad to see what had been a working farm reduced to nothing more than a common dump. The place is littered with abandoned washing machines, rubber tyres and ancient drinks cans.

The grounds were one thing but I gasp when I see the house. Specks of white cling to the outside walls, but the paint had been stripped back by the weather and years of neglect. The roof has caved in on one side, leaving rafters exposed. Most of the glass in the windows has either fallen out or been smashed by vandals. Childish graffiti is scrawled over the front door, which lies on the ground unhinged. I stop on the threshold and recoil at the dusty stench of a dead building.

Inside, some of the furniture remains, but it's dilapidated and rotten. Chairs are burnt and what's left of the plaster sags precariously on the walls. And yet, despite all that, it's still good to be back. The feel of the building remains intact and the sense of love I have for the place will never change.

Sifting through the rubble in the kitchen I peer through a hole in the wall to the living room. I remember sitting there with my Gran in front of a roaring fire, with tall tales helping to get us through the cold winters of the early 80s. My smile fades. Everything changed when my parents disappeared.

Suddenly, upstairs there's a loud crash, which startles me. Maybe I've disturbed someone? I'm not sure what to do so I just stand there and listen. My stomach turns when a screech pierces through the murk of the cottage. Despite a pressing urge to leave, I know I can't go. I make up my mind to investigate the top floor.

Outside a car stops nearby but I decide it's nothing and press on. Looking at the stairs I'm not convinced they're safe. The banister's hanging off and when I tentatively test my weight on the first step the wood sags. Even so, I think I might be able to get up if I'm careful. Slowly, I use the outside of the steps to make my way up, and although wood disintegrates underfoot in places, it's not enough to stop me.

Upstairs, the rooms are even worse. Floorboards in the smaller bedroom have collapsed and I grab on to the door frame to stop myself from falling through. My Gran's old room is just the same, with graffiti covering what remains of the wallpaper, too wet to make out in the gloom.

Whatever I'd hoped to find, it's not here. A gentle buzz in my bag alerts me to a new message and glancing at my phone I see that my brother's arrived.

I'm waiting for you outside

I nod. For once he's managed to get me at exactly the right time.

Nuggets

Sandy Stirrit pulled up outside Gillian Casselly's cottage, just off the busy main road. He was weaving his way to Maggie, but he needed more background to complete the big picture. Gillian Casselly had been quoted in the press back in the 80s and Sandy thought she might still be able to give him something new, a thread that others had missed.

Unsure of the reception he'd get, Sandy knocked and waited. He was greeted by a woman in her forties with a furrowed brow and a worried look. He smiled and introduced himself. The mention of his press credentials prompted Gillian to start closing the door.

'Please Gillian, just two minutes of your time,' said Sandy.

Gillian hesitated, the recognition of her name enough to make her stop, if only for a second. Sandy took his opportunity, 'I saw Maggie Balfour recently and she didn't seem well. You knew her better than anyone once.'

Gillian stopped and nodded, 'Why's this all coming back out now?'

Sandy wasn't 100% sure what she meant but he kept talking, 'I think she wants to tie-up some loose ends, but there's more to this than that. I think you might be able to help?'

Gillian was shaking her head, 'I, I don't want to get back into it. It was hard to take at the time and when I saw her, well the old wounds still haven't healed. I thought she might have mellowed, but she's just the same.'

Sandy gestured inside, 'Do you mind if I come in?'

Gillian opened the door and Sandy sloped past. In the living room the reporter sat down and waited for his host to say something, but he ended up filling the silence with another question, 'So, have you seen her recently?' Gillian nodded but apparently had nothing to add. Sandy persisted. 'I saw her at the event for her great uncle. You know, the World War One thing? She seemed quite,' Sandy hesitated, trying to find the right word, 'agitated.' He paused, 'Does that sound fair?' Gillian was still nodding. 'The thing is she doesn't seem quite herself; she acted very strangely and left the event midway.' Sandy stopped, failing to find clues in her face, he tried a different approach. 'Maggie started screaming in the middle of her speech which caused quite a stir I can tell you.' Sandy was smiling, trying to make a personal connection with Gillian but was coming up blank. 'It's just that with everything that happened in the past, I'm not sure how stable she is and what she might do.' Still Gillian had nothing to say. 'So what I want to know is has she actually said anything to you about what happened in the 80s?'

The pair sat in silence. Gillian lit a cigarette and inhaled deeply before she spoke, the smoke billowing from her mouth, clouding her face as the words finally crept out.

'It all started to go wrong for her after her parents went missing. As you'll probably know they were last seen not far from here, up at Threepwood.' Gillian gestured out of the window towards the hills. 'They'd been scattering her Gran's ashes; but her Mum and Dad were never seen again. They just didn't come home.' Gillian examined her cigarette as the ash lengthened, momentarily defying gravity before flaking down on the hardwood floor. She brushed it away absentmindedly with her slippers. 'Can you imagine losing both of your parents at the same time and then finding out nothing more about it?' Sandy took notes but only nodded, 'There was a fire at the Rocking Stone that day but there was no-one there. They searched for days but there was nothing to see, no bodies, nothing at all. Can you imagine what that would do to the children left behind, both desperate for news? Poor Maggie didn't know how to take it. She wanted to take care of her brother but they were just kids and they ended up being put into a children's home. I didn't recognise her after that. She went off the rails, lashed out at everyone that tried to help. Drinking and fighting at school, all that sort of stuff. I stuck by her at first, she was my best friend after all – but in the end it was her who left me.'

Sandy was trying to read the situation. He'd seen most of this detail before and was looking to dig out a golden nugget – something new, 'When was the last time you saw her before she left for Canada?'

'The day she turned up in the car,' Gillian's voice was almost inaudible and Sandy had to lean in to hear what she said. 'She was drunk driving a car she'd stolen from old Joe – he was a family friend, God bless him, and long gone now. She was going to the coast. She said she wanted me to come but I was scared. Later on, I found out that she'd gone to meet her brother. She picked him up from a football game and things unravelled from then.'

'So what did you do?'

Gillian was stubbing out her cigarette. She looked back at Sandy with a new composure, 'I begged her to get out of the car and come to speak to my Mum. My Mum was still here then and I was sure she could have helped, but of course Maggie wouldn't listen. She said I was a coward and no fun. When she drove off I never saw her again. Not until she came back this week.'

Sandy had been busy writing. He stopped and looked up, 'Was she different to how you remembered?'

'When I first saw her, my heart leapt. I thought it was my Maggie and I've missed her so much over the years. She was my first best friend and it was a big wrench to be left on my own. It took me years to find that trust again. But the more she said, the more the good memories faded. I saw that Maggie hadn't changed at all.'

'And how did that make you feel?' Sandy had heard enough to vindicate his idea that Maggie had returned home with ulterior motives. He repeated the question, 'How did it make you feel to see Maggie Balfour after all these years?'

Gillian looked directly at Sandy and spoke with no hesitation, 'I was scared. I didn't know what she'd do or why she'd come. All that was left was anger.'

Return to the Rocking Stone

I found Martin waiting outside, sitting on the window sill. He was staring down towards the reservoir and at first I wasn't sure if he'd heard me. I cough before speaking, trying to get his attention and he turns and smiles. 'I saw you at the ceremony yesterday, Martin, but you didn't do anything to help.' He nods. 'You left me there to deal with them all; you should have stayed. I felt such a fool.'

'You needed to do that by yourself,' said Martin, shifting uncomfortably.

'I came all the way from Canada to represent the family!'

'No you didn't,' Martin raised his voice, 'Charlie was Grandad's brother, yeah, they both grew up near here,' he said, gesturing around, 'but could they have been any more different? Davie worked the land, while Charlie drank himself to death – but no one wants to talk about that, do they?'

I'm trying to process what he's saying, it doesn't make sense. I'm trying to figure it all out when Martin breaks my chain of thought, 'I mean, we never even met him; he was dead before we were born.'

It was too much and I tell him what I know, 'I saw Charlie yesterday, in the woods. He tried to kill me; with his rifle.'

Martin looks at me coldly and laughs, 'You'd like to think so wouldn't you. It would make all this just a little easier.'

There was something off with his eyes that I couldn't quite place, a new kind of hatred, which scares me.

'Martin, why did you come here?'

'Because you wanted me to come.'

'But I didn't ask you.'

'You didn't have to. We both know that there's something we need to do.'

We look up to Cuff Hill and move closer together. I can feel his breath on my face, 'I think we should retrace Mum and Dad's last steps and go back up to the Rocking Stone; maybe it will help put all these years of grief to rest?'

I nod and we walk off back down the drive and back out onto the open road. From the order of service that was left behind we had a note of our parents' movements on the day they vanished. They'd scattered Gran's ashes at the Rocking Stone after stopping at the druids' graves. It was an easy path, but for the life of me I can't seem to find the way. The route I knew from childhood was blocked by a tall barbed-wire deer fence, which ran right along the road as far as the eye could see. Scanning the perimeter there's no obvious way of getting through.

'What now?' asks Martin.

'We'll need to try and get round it somehow.' I walk off along the road and back up the hill towards town. Eventually we come to a metal gate which opens out into the field below Cuff Hill. The once-open pasture had been heavily planted with pine trees, making the way up to the stone hard to navigate, with the trees planted in deep rolling drainage troughs. It had been raining and each depression had turned into a trickling stream. As I start the steep climb I struggle to keep my balance, while Martin quickly finds his feet and strides ahead. About 15 minutes later we reach the clearing.

The enclosure around the Rocking Stone had fallen to ruin, with the dry stone perimeter wall all but flattened. It looked like cattle had trampled the earth around the stone to a muddy bog, while many of the remaining circle of birch trees were rotting in the sodden earth. It's a shadow of the place I remembered.

'Well this isn't looking too promising, is it sis?'

I ignore him. Martin was always negative about our parents' disappearance. He thinks they left because they couldn't cope with the responsibility of bringing us up, but I was sure something had happened to them and was determined to find out what. I wade through the mud, making my way closer to the stone which I can now almost touch. Glancing back, I see Martin waiting by the perimeter wall, 'You're on your own this time,' he said, 'but I'll be waiting for you, don't worry about that.'

I curse him again and lean forward to try and reach the stone. I lose one of my shoes in the mud in the process, but I persist. I think back to the stories my Gran used to tell us around the fire. She tried to scare us with tales of the Lady of Threepwood and while I'd never believed them, she put so much energy into her performance that they were always fun to hear.

It all seems so long ago. My heart's still pounding from the effort of the climb. I've never felt so tired. With some effort I manage to raise myself from the bog to a square of raised turf and finally come face-to-face with the stone. The weather had changed and it felt much colder. I can see my warm breath conjure shapes in the autumn air. Slowly, I reach out and place my hand on the stone; waiting for some sudden clue, a bolt from the blue, but there's nothing. In the background Martin chides me again, 'See, I told you there was nothing here.' A wind's getting up and the hairs on the nape of my neck stand on end. Suddenly a strong gust completely takes my breath away.

As if stepping into a storm, gale force winds pin me to the stone and I struggle to maintain my balance. I turn again and cry out for my brother, but he's nowhere to be seen. The gnawing sensation in my stomach is back with a vengeance. I become aware of a dull groaning above me, which quickly switches to a sharp crack. When I finally look up I see a dark shape fall, but it's too late to move.

I feel sick and weak at the knees. Suddenly, the world changes; fire burns around me with a thunderous roar. I'm still standing in the centre of the stone circle, but the wall's been rebuilt and the ground around me is flat and dry. Looking down, I see my clothes aflame but I feel no pain. Looking in horror at my burning hands I try to scream but can't. Then, as quickly as it had appeared, the fire draws back and someone steps through. Squinting, I feel fear like never before. A cloaked figure is moving slowly towards me, its face covered by thick white robes, the flames dissipating from its body with every step.

'Leave me alone, just let me go,' I scream, but it keeps coming, stopping inches away. I gasp as it slowly pulls back the cowl with both hands. My fingers are scratching at the stone as I try to block out this ghoulish vision. Instead, my finger nails splinter under the pressure. I don't want to look, but I can't turn away. Tears stream down my face. I can't believe what I'm seeing. I look again and I couldn't be more certain. I smile at my mother and memories flood back of better days. I never thought I would see her face again. My happiness is short lived and when she speaks it's only to reject me.

'No' she screams; her body somehow transforming, warping and bending to twice its size, gnarling into new shapes as the flames take hold once more. A loud piercing explosion cracks above me and I'm thrown to the ground.

When I come to, I'm back in the clearing, pinned down by two branches that had fallen from a tree overhanging the Rocking Stone.

Slow progress

Sandy Stirrit was fourth in line at a drive-thru Costa when Gillian Casselly phoned him back. He was surprised to hear from her. Gillian had already confirmed the details he wanted and Sandy was ready to put his questions directly to Maggie. Intrigued, he scanned the waiting cars and decided to take the call, 'Hi, Sandy Stirrit speaking; how can I help you?'

There was a moment's hesitation; the sound of a crackling cigarette was followed by the gentle hiss of smoke hitting the receiver. It seemed that Gillian was still happy to bide her time, 'You were round seeing me earlier today at the house.' Sandy nodded but said nothing; he knew that this time the caller would fill the silence.

'I think Maggie might be in trouble,' said Gillian.

'I think we both know there's something wrong.' Sandy had the phone cradled in his neck and moved up a space in the queue. Gillian kept talking.

'The last time I saw her; not now, I mean back in the 80s, she drove off down to the coast; drunk in the car with her brother.'

'I remember seeing the coverage.' In truth Sandy had spent the last few days pouring over old newspaper clippings and archive footage.

'When she left my house she was agitated. I mean I'd never seen her quite like that before. I told you that she'd threatened me, but when she left she took a call. She'd mentioned her brother had been trying to contact her when I tried to help her. But outside she was—'

'—you could hear her?'

'Not everything, no, but I could hear enough. She said was she was going to the coast; that she wanted to meet her brother back at the beach.'

'So, you're worried?'

'I don't know what she's thinking, but I do know that nothing good's ever going to come of her going back to Portencross. The last time she was there; well, she never really recovered.'

There was silence for a few seconds. Gillian took another draw from her cigarette, holding the smoke deep in her lungs, before she continued. 'Another thing, too. After you came round, I took a call from Canada. It was a friend of hers, Darcie Fen, who'd tracked me down online. She said that Maggie had mentioned me a few times recently. She wanted to know if I'd heard from her. I didn't know what to say.'

Sandy was listening with interest, but he wasn't sure what Gillian wanted him to do. 'This sounds like a job for the Police?'

Gillian hesitated before replying, 'I'm scared to phone them; maybe it's nothing. I don't want her to get into more trouble than she's already in. She's ill, though, she needs our help.'

Sandy paused before probing a little deeper, 'Did she say when she wanted to meet her brother?'

'She didn't say exactly; she just said to meet her at the same place at the same time. It hadn't even occurred to me when I saw her but today's the anniversary of the incident on the beach. Whatever it is that's in her head, I think it's going to happen soon.'

The receiver clicked off. Sandy wasn't sure what to do. He looked at his watch: 1pm. If Maggie was planning on revisiting her past he had less than two hours to get his act together.

Bogged down

The branches are heavy with water but rotten right through and I push them off and throw them back in the mire. Winded, I sit with my back against the Rocking Stone and scan the clearing looking for my brother, but he's gone. Raising myself to all fours I crawl through the mud until I'm back on solid ground. It's raining heavily and the water's slowly washing the filth from me, rivulets of brown earth turning to liquid and running off into the bog. I'm still shaking from my vision but I knew it couldn't have been real; my mother was long gone. The drugs I'd been taking were strong and I knew there were side effects. Up until now I'd always believed my visions were false, but now I wasn't so sure.

Slowly, I make my way back down Cuff Hill. I spot my car by the road near the farm, but there's still no sign of Martin. In the distance, I hear the drone of a car heading west. I knew that at times I'd been unkind to my brother but I'd always tried to help when I could; even if he didn't really understand me. Cursing him, I try clumsily to navigate the gorse, grabbing the rough branches of the young pine trees to try and keep my balance. The trickle of water that had been running through the planting trenches had grown to a steady flow and I fall more than once before reaching the safety of the waiting tarmac.

I scan the horizon, knowing that I'd survive the ghosts this place conjured up. The day of my parents' disappearance had hit me like a tonne of bricks. I couldn't face reliving it all again today, not when I feel like this. I start to cough in the rain and cover my mouth with my hands to try and catch the blood which I'm finding it harder to stem. I know I don't have much time to make things right. I need to find answers; to put my mind at rest and to make sure my brother knows that I've always been there for him.

I sit in the car, wet and miserable until the truth finally dawns on me. I smile when I realise that we will meet again and soon – he'd promised to be there, back at the beach. I turn on the engine and drive off, my speed increasing as country lanes give way to main roads. Memories flit by like passing cars and I feel better than I have in months. Just this one last thing to do, then I can finally move on.

Closing in

Sandy Stirrit phoned John, his friend on the force, to sound him out about his plans for Maggie Balfour. He hadn't liked the response. John told him that he had little to act on; that there were no official complaints and that, on the face of it, Maggie had done nothing wrong. Sandy argued that there was more to Maggie than met the eye; that he felt she knew more about the series of disappearances that had plagued her family than she'd let on. His friend was unconvinced, though, and warned Sandy about the consequences of getting involved in something that was none of his business. Sandy hung up, amazed at how little his friend understood journalists.

About an hour later Sandy drove to the beach. He wound down the narrow, single-track road which led to a gorse-lined car park overlooking the Clyde estuary. It was 2:30pm, about an hour before the press reports suggested the previous incident had taken place.

There were already a few other cars parked up; most likely left by dog walkers. One rusted heap looked like it had been dumped some time ago, its windows thick with sea salt and sand, blown in from the coast. Sandy had no idea if any of the cars were Maggie's but he knew that if she was coming then she wouldn't be far away.

Climbing up the dunes, navigating the tall marram grass, Sandy stopped to scan the horizon. At first the beach looked empty. It was bright and hard to see and there were no obvious signs of life. Then, through the haze, he saw shadows dancing on the sand. Someone was there, looking out to sea. Raising his hand to try and block out the light, Sandy squinted through the glare, but he couldn't see clearly. Waves crashed off outlying rocks, almost drowning out the sound of distant gulls, while strong winds drove sand from the pristine beach in shifting sheets towards him, making it hard to see. Sandy sensed his moment had arrived and zig-zagged through the dunes and down to the beach. He waved at the far-off shadows and shouted as loud as he could in the vain hope that he might be heard.

Back on the beach

Martin was true to his word and we met back on the beach for the first time in nearly 30 years. We took our time, ambling slowly across the sand reminiscing about our childhood and some of the things we'd missed after we'd been split up and put into care. Seagulls hovered in mid-air, hoping to claim scraps of food but there were slim pickings on that front. As we drew closer to the shoreline the conversation tailed off, the water lapping nearer with the coming high tide. The sea was lively and waves crashed into the outlying rocky islands.

It was Martin who eventually broke the silence, 'It's been a long time since we've been here, sis. Why now?'

I couldn't look at him and watched the waves; my mind flashed with images from our last visit. 'I think it's time we talked about that day; so much happened. We just swept it all away, like a guilty secret.' I turn to my brother, a good man with prospects; everything I could ever have wanted in a sibling. It's hard for me to say what I need him to hear. 'Martin, I know I owe you an apology.' He's shaking his head and fighting back tears, the past so hard to bear, even now.

Behind him in the distance I spot a man in black walking across the sand. He's waving but I can't be sure if he's trying to get my attention or just struggling to see. For some reason it makes me nervous and I turn back to my brother. It's now or never.

'I'll be quick, Martin, but please know that despite everything that happened that day I have, and always will, love you – more than anyone else on this lousy planet. You'll always be my little brother.'

I turn away again and he starts to laugh; the grating sound slowly drowned out by the crashing waves.

1988

I'd been living in Maryfield Children's Home for years and had hated every second. Overcrowded and noisy, it took all my powers just to try and shut it all out. Today had been worse than normal and it was barely past breakfast. I reach for my headphones and switch on the cassette, heavy metal filling the void and keeping the world at bay. I close my eyes and lie back on the bed. How much longer will I need to stay here? Just because I'm older, no-one wants to look after me. They say I've a reputation for being difficult; that after five years I should accept my folks are gone and move on.

It's easy for them to say. My brother had been luckier; people liked him and he was younger which made him easier to 'place'. The lucky bugger had been adopted quickly and he liked his new life with Jim and Elaine. Martin said he'd tried to get them to take me too, but they thought that taking on two was too much. I think they'd considered it early on. They'd visited once. I think that's what put them off – they should have known what to expect. Martin said it had been my loss. He'd been right about that.

The guitar solo kicks in and I turn up the volume. At the same time the door bursts open and Helen and Gary tumble into my room. They're the two oldest kids here and they run riot, not caring who gets in their way. Helen grabs my feet and starts to pull me from the bed while Gary rolls me off. It's not the first time we've fought. I fall awkwardly onto the floor and they start punching me, laughing, demanding I hand over my Walkman. No way. It's one of the only things I've got left from Mum and they're not getting it without a fight. I held it close to my chest, away from their greedy fingers. They drag me into the corner of the room and pin me down. I can't get up but I won't give in. I launch off the wall, my back arching painfully as I try to stand. Then suddenly I go limp and slump to the floor and they lose their hold. I grip the Walkman as hard as I can and lash out, swinging again and again until they stop. I run from the home and keep going. I won't be back.

Later I had to decide what to do and sought the unwitting help of a family friend. Joe was the only person from the old days who still kept in touch. He came round to see me every so often and we went out for coke and sometimes a movie. He was ancient, though, and we didn't have much to say to each other. He'd known my Mum well, though, and it was good to be able to ask him about her and to keep her memory alive. Old Joe lived in a small cottage in the middle of nowhere. I knew he was away today, off out with a friend on a coach trip up north, which meant his car was free. The silly old goat didn't have much of a head for security. He kept spare house keys under a rock in his garden. It's the most obvious stone you could imagine; painted blue and sat right next to the door. Looking around to make sure no-one saw me, I turn it over, snatch the keys, and let myself in. His car keys are hanging in the usual place in the kitchen. I can feel a thirst coming on and a devil's on my shoulder, looking for lager and wine. After raiding his drinks cabinet I make for the garage. My summer days driving tractors at Threepwood were finally going to count for something. I open one of the bottles and drink deeply, grimacing at the acrid taste but enjoying the way it makes me feel. I slot the keys into the Land Rover's ignition and fire up the engine. After a few false starts I'm off. A pit stop at a friend's house proves to be a waste of time, so I carry on solo. It's time my brother learned how the other half live.

Martin's adoption had bagged him a move to a massive house on the coast and that's where I'm heading. I keep a low profile driving through the small towns on the way and arrive in Largs about half an hour later. Martin plays football on Saturdays and I drive to the local park and wait. After the game finishes he passes the car while talking to a friend. Martin's wearing the yellow smiley face t-shirt I gave him for his birthday. I roll down the window and shout him over, 'Hey Martin; how you doing?'

Martin looks at his pal and then nervously back at me, 'It's alright, Peter, I'll catch up with you later.' Peter smiles and leaves. I can see that my brother's not happy.

'What the hell do you think you're doing driving this?' He casts his eyes over the car, trying to place it, 'Its Joe's isn't it? I'd recognise it anywhere.'

'He said I could use it, but I'm not here to argue. Get in.'

We both had very different personalities but I knew Martin would do as he was told; he was scared of me. Not long after we left town and started heading down the coast.

By the time we arrive at Portencross it's early afternoon. I park the car in the grassy area bounded by marram grass and dunes.

Taking out a six pack of beer I pass a can to my brother, 'This is for you.' He looks at the can with disgust and shakes his head, but I won't take no for an answer. 'You do drink, don't you?'

'Of course I do,' he said, but when he gagged on the first sip I knew he was lying. We sit there drinking until there's nothing left. He's laughing now and more relaxed. I suggest we take a trip along the beach and he's out of the car and off like a dog let loose from its lead. I run after him but I'm out of breath by the time we reach the sea.

'Looks cold in there, sis' he said. Looking back at me with his clean cut, calm expression reminds me why I'm here; of how much I resent his cosy wee life, with barely a thought for his big sister.

'Why don't we chance it and go for a swim?' I say. Martin looks at me like I'm crazy, 'Not far, just out to those rocks,' I continue, pointing to a large outcrop a couple of hundred metres off the beach.

'Oh, I don't know, sis. It looks pretty rough out there, and I'm not as good in the water as you.'

I'd made up my mind and won't take no for an answer. I start to strip to my underwear. 'Rubbish, I bet you get back to shore quicker than me. I'll race you.'

The challenge gives him the confidence he needs and Martin pulls off the yellow smiley faced t-shirt he treasures so much, and not long after I watch as he plunges headlong into the surf.

We swim together for a while but the waves are hard to navigate and I can feel the currents tug at me; trying to sweep me out to sea. I stop swimming to tread water when I notice Martin's in trouble. He's calling out for me, bobbing up and down at the waterline. I know he can't see where I am. This is it. Treading water in the rough sea I count slowly to 100. When I stop, my brother's nowhere to be seen. I smile. It had been too easy.

Though the waves were crashing hard against the rocks I manage to swim to the rocky outcrop and climb up, cutting myself badly, my surf-soaked body collapsing on the rocks where I lie exhausted for hours. I'm found the next morning, after the storm. A beach comber had seen our clothes on the sand and heard my screams for help.

It had been a big deal. The papers wanted to know where Martin was and the reporters kept asking what happened. I tell them that I can't remember and that the whole thing had just been an awful nightmare.

I've been saying it ever since.

The Cold, Black Sea

Nothing had changed. I feel as empty about it now as I had back then. I'd hated Martin for being able to switch off and forget about our family. I resented the fact that he'd found a happy home. He needed to pay.

I knew the currents were strong on this stretch of coast and the only thing I'd wanted was a sense of justice. He was right, I was a better swimmer than him. In the end they said he'd just got lost. His body was never found. In the end it had been put down as nothing more than a terrible accident.

I left the country as soon as I was old enough and I didn't look back. Or maybe I'd always looked back but hadn't realised until now; caught in my own private hell. Part of me still wants to believe that it really had been nothing more than good fun gone wrong. I don't know what to think anymore. One thing's for sure, though, karma's a bitch; and cancer was the calling card to bring me home.

It was about the time of my diagnosis that I'd started talking to Martin again. Back on the beach I turn to tell my brother that I'm sorry, but he's vanished. The only person there is a figure in black, waving at me in the distance. He's much closer now and I realise it's the journalist that had come after me at Charlie's memorial.

I wasn't sure how long I'd been standing in the sea, but the tide was well in and I was standing thigh-deep in water; the waves chilling my legs and lapping past to shore.

As I watch the water rise, I'm gripped by my latest attack. Excruciating pain pulses through every sinew, causing white pin-pricks of light to pierce my eyes; postcards from a deadly disease. A sharp pain shoots down my left side and I collapse headfirst into the sea.

***

When Sandy Stirrit saw Maggie fall he ran as fast as he could. Fierce winds lashed sand at him, blinding him for precious seconds. Shielding his eyes he pressed on, but by the time he had reached the water, Maggie was gone.

***

As the waves engulf me I see Martin as he had been all those years ago; 12 years old, wearing a white t-shirt with a yellow smiley face. He looks at me through the murky sea and grins. Suddenly, a wave sweeps him from sight and when he reappears he's changed. All I see now is the horror I created when I'd destroyed my brother on a whim.

Martin's decayed, bloated corpse surfaces for a split-second, before the force of the tide takes him away from me for the final time. My mouth is open. I try to scream but can't. I watch as my brother's fetid remains disintegrate against the same razor sharp rocks that I'd taken refuge on all those years ago, the metal pole still there to warn off the reckless.

There's nothing left. I slip under, choking on the water and brace myself for the worst. Sinking deeper I accept my fate and let go, finally surrendering to the call of the cold, black sea.

About the author

Originally from Ayrshire, Campbell Hart lives in Glasgow with his wife, Lisa, and their two boys.

A qualified broadcast journalist he's been a professional writer for more than twenty years in commercial radio, BBC Scotland, and for various public and private sector organisations.

Other books by the author include the crime fiction trilogy featuring DI John Arbogast (Wilderness, The Nationalist, and Referendum). The novels were all bestsellers on the Amazon Noir chart.

Fresh crime fiction is currently in the pipeline.

For more details visit: www.campbellhart.co.uk

Acknowledgements

The Sniper: The Sniper is a work of fiction and in no way looks to do a disservice to any of those involved in that bloodiest of conflicts. For further reading I would recommend Richard Van Emden's 'The Somme' which provided a real flavour of what it was like for ordinary soldiers serving at the Somme. This book does not set out to tell their stories, but details from the letters and accounts provided did inspire part of the narrative of the story you've just read.

The Rocking Stone: There is very little information available on who the druids actually were, with that fundamental mystery going to the very heart of this tale. However, for further reading I would recommend Jean Markale's 'The Druids – Celtic Priests of Nature' – the book offers interesting insights into the way druids faded into obscurity with the onset of Christianity, while casting some light onto their customs and worldview.

A new edition of 'The grand grimoire – the red dragon' as edited by Tarl Warwick is available online. Parts of the Rocking Stone are inspired from the text which is taken from the notorious original which exploded into public life in 1750.

The Rocking Stone itself can be found off the A737 in the Bigholm hills near Beith, Ayrshire. If you're feeling brave, travel up Threepwood Road and look for the circle of trees on top of Cuff Hill!

The Cold, Black Sea: A book that emerged from the debris of the first two, the glue which holds it all together flowed from the Lou Reed album 'Magic and Loss'.

Thanks

This collection was inspired by the work of M.R James, too much cheese and wine, and a mental nudge from old friend and long-time collaborator, Tim Byrne.

A special mention to my other half, Lisa, who helped me to finally get this book over the line, despite the demands of a young family. I appreciate your encouragement!

Finally, I'd also like to thank Marjorie Calder and Rosie McIntosh for your critical eyes and constructive feedback through the years. Indie authors rely on their networks and without your help the process of unravelling plot points would have taken so much longer.

CH, 2020

Printed in Great Britain
by Amazon

47507922R00111